Massacre of the Innocents.

For what must have been a very long time, I crawled on the floor like a child, touching every cold stone, while silently begging forgiveness from each child buried below. No names were carved into the rock, but I know some would certainly have been my playmates. Their young souls were freed when their lives ended, while mine remains hidden away in a crypt of my own making, buried deep within my heart.

WWW.TOMTRUJILLO.COM

COVER PAINTING: JESUS, THE TEENAGE YEARS
BY TOM TRUJILLO

COVER AND BOOK DESIGN BY TOM TRUJILLO

FICTION
ISBN-13: 978-1534776463
ISBN-10: 153477646x

HERESY

JESUS, THE TEENAGE YEARS

A LOVE STORY

BY

TOM TRUJILLO

No one knows that I passed the crisis of adolescence
at the ludicrous age of thirteen years.
A crisis which has no medical name
but the knowing might call generalized tumescence.
I was swollen with garbage and bitterness,
and saw no possibility of relief in a world
of grubbing hypocrisy and greed.
My own ego was monstrous,
mainly because I had never done anything
for anyone and could justify my uselessness
only by assuming that the world was not worth my energy.

teenage jesus
Ricardo Means Ybarra

THE HERETIC

Inspiration came to the artist on a lazy afternoon as he thought about his son, and how similar his story paralleled that of Jesus as told in the Bible. First, there was the glorious birth followed by the magical childhood before separating from the family at the age of thirteen. It seems that's the age when the child discovers that mom isn't a virgin but had a boyfriend before she and dad got married. And Dad is not a God but only works as a tile setter for some ass who thinks he's God. The artist wondered why the Bible had omitted Jesus' teenage years. When asking others about this oversight, most blinked in confusion as if waking from a stupor before answering, "That's odd; I've never thought about that before."

The artist began searching through dozens of art history books for any painting of a young adult Jesus and was shocked to find absolutely nothing. From DaVinci, Michelangelo, Raphael, Rembrandt, and everyone else, nobody that he knew of had ever created a painting of Jesus at the age of seventeen or eighteen.

Puzzled by the absence of any depiction of Jesus as a young adult, the artist was overjoyed by the thought of creating a truly unique narrative on one of history's most popular religious figures in a period of his life that had been overlooked by nearly everyone for over two thousand years.

"Who are you? To portray Jesus as a rebel implies a separation from His DEITY. Jesus I can assure you, is, was, and will always be greater than we are, were, or will ever be. We need to let Him make us, not us make Him. We have a propensity to be the "rebel" until at what point The Holy Spirit is welcomed to change us, that we may follow Jesus and worship in spirit and truth. Your painting is blasphemy!"

Reverend Eugene Cranston, Pine Valley, Idaho

OPENING NIGHT

The phone springs to life just before the morning cup of coffee reaches my awaiting lips. I ignore the repetitive sound of wind chimes and close my eyes, taking in the satisfying flavor of the rich taste of. Still, it's 7 am. Who in the hell calls anyone at this hour?

I cast a sour look at the illuminated name displayed on the phone and see Anita's name, the art gallery coordinator of a new group show I'm a part of. Tonight is the opening, and a new show is always a momentous occasion for the gallery, the artists, and the community, so I pick up the phone in case it's important. But still, it's too early to be calling me.

"David? Have you been on your computer or seen today's paper?" she asks excitedly.

"No, I just woke up."

"Sorry about that. I hope you at least got some coffee in."

Anita sounds like she's already two cups ahead of me. "Some of your art is causing quite a stir," she warns me with a laugh. "Read the letters to the editor section. There's one written by a Reverend Eugene Cranston. He's not too thrilled about one of your paintings."

"I can only guess which one it might be," I laugh.

"The press has already warned me they'll be there to cover it. You better be prepared!"

Be prepared...for what? Maybe I should get the paper.

Ten hours later, Sidney and I turn the corner and spot a large crowd milling about on the sidewalk in front of the gallery. I hope these aren't friends of the Reverend, the irate letter writer leading a mob of the faithful to run me out of town.

Sidney calms me with a firm grasp of my arm and a beaming smile, "Look at all your new fans waiting to meet you!"

"Yeah, or to burn me at the stake."

Fortunately for me, the blasphemer, I look pretty much like everyone else and we're able to pass into the gallery unnoticed and unmolested. Once we're safely inside, I'm bowled over by the intensity of the noisy, animated crowd—a gallery opening is a gay social event and the community is out in full force. I notice that the walls are hung with the usual abstract and impressionist works, but I begin to worry when I don't see any of my paintings. Maybe Anita was pressured into removing them.

Sidney can read me like a book. "I'll get us some wine," she says patting me on the back. "Go see if you can find your paintings."

I trudge through the gallery and stop in front of a few large canvases featuring formless layers of colors haphazardly splashed in all directions, but held together by thin, black, geometric lines. An art critic might say, "The artist has moved away from paint as the star of the work toward a less gestural, more hard-edged form." I do a quick survey of all the works by this artist and I like them, but I'm distracted and in search of my work. Nearing the rear of the gallery I still haven't located my stuff and I'm becoming more insecure than usual.

I turn around when I feel an arm touch my shoulder and am greeted by Anita. She leans in close so as not to draw any unwanted attention and whispers, "Oh my God, your work is so fabulous!"

"Where are they?"

"At the top of the main landing. I think you'll be very happy!"

Four steps from the second-floor landing I can see the frames meticulously hung in alignment and at the top of the stairs I pause and take a deep breath, or maybe it's a gasp. The paintings fill the entire width of a long, well-lit wall and wrap around another wall in sort of an L-shape. Three or four people are looking at each painting, and Jesus, The Teenage Years, has a large crowd gathered around it, including a couple of news photographers.

As I Look at the collection in its entirety, I suddenly realize I don't remember doing them. I worked long and hard with each one, I do know that. But nothing went smoothly until a certain moment when everything began to flow almost effortlessly. Whatever I had been struggling with previously, would take shape without me being aware of how it occurred. This transition, from frustration to effortless abandon is still a mystery to me. Sometimes just smearing two or three colors together formed a face, or a beard partially wiped off, which became the shaved head on another figure. I've heard this from other artists too—every painting is a struggle until, at some point, it stops being so. I lean against the railing and wonder, when did I become the viewer and no longer the artist?

I'm still talking to myself when Christine, Mark, and art Carla walk up the stairs and I say lamely, "Pretty good turnout, don't you think?"

"Have you noticed which artist is getting all the attention?" replies Carla. "You are what's happening in the art world because abstract and modern is passé. Historical, narrative, figurative art is where it's at, and that is what you are doing."

I make a mental note to remember this the next time anyone asks me what kind of art I make. I think of myself as a storyteller, making commentaries on myths, human behavior, or man versus nature. Hopefully, all with a sense of irony. Inspiration comes when I least expect it, such as what happened after watching the play La Virgen de Tepiyac, and I ended up with a painting titled, The Virgin of Smallpox.

"I'm surprised how the colors gain in intensity the further you get from your paintings," remarks Christine. She steps in for a closer look at The Virgin of Smallpox and studies the details before turning back to me. "Someday you'll have to explain this to me, but I love the narrow format, which is much like the narrow-minded thinking of the Catholic Church."

"Can I use that line?" I joke.

I love it when a viewer finds something in my work that I've never considered. In the case of The Virgin of Smallpox, a narrow piece of birch wood panel was drafted into action because that's what I had lying around the studio. I knew exactly what I wanted to paint and there was none of the usual preliminary drawings. I sketched out a quick idea on notebook paper and went directly to a charcoal sketch on the board.

Mark leans in and whispers, "Is Teenage Jesus still for sale? I'd like to surprise Christine for her birthday."

Before I can answer him, a well-dressed attractive woman pushes her way past Mark and clenches my forearm in a vise grip. She pulls me aside and gives Mark and Christine an aggressive, toothy smile. "I need to talk to the artist if you don't mind. It's deadline time."

"Come on you two," says Carla to Christine and Mark. "Let's let the artist get to work."

Before they leave, Mark leans in and whispers, "Seriously, David, give me a call about Teenage Jesus."

Christine softly elbows the woman aside, kisses me on the cheek, and says, "We plan to be the new de'Medicis, and we want to start our collection with a commission. Call me next week."

Christine smiles at the woman as she turns to go, and says, "Hi Robyn! We've met before, remember? You did a spread on our house last year, the one you titled, California Dreamin?"

Robyn stutters out a reply, "Oh yes, I do recall it. The one surrounded by olive trees?"

"It was a very nice piece," smiles Christine and smiles and quickly leaves with Mark and Carla.

"Do you know those guys?" I ask.

Robyn searches her memory and replies, "Christina, right? She caught me by surprise, but I do remember the house. Quite a beauty! You know, I do so many articles it's difficult to remember them all."

Robyn turns to me and leans in close. "Okay, so listen...David ...my name is Robyn Harris, and I'm with Coastal Style Magazine. Do you have time to talk? Just a few questions and I'll let you get back to this wonderful reception. By the way, congratulations, you seem to be the talk of the town!"

Robyn takes my hand and guides me over the paintings and we stand in front of *Jesus, The Teenage Years*. She studies the handsome, dark-skinned, young Jesus walking through an ancient town square with a beautiful young woman. Her face is painted white and she's wearing a headband of gold coins. I added a tattoo on Jesus' stomach that spells out APOSTLES in old script, and all in caps favored by today's gang-bangers. When she saw the painting, Sidney laughed at the lettering after having listened to me complain for years about anyone using all capitals with an Old English decorative font.

"This is tongue-in-cheek, right?" asks Robyn. "I mean, did you paint this to intentionally insult and rile up Christians?"

"Not at all. There was no conscious intention on my part to provoke anyone," I laugh. "The title itself is pretty funny though, don't you think? But it's merely a modern term for the ages between thirteen and nineteen—a little levity never hurt anyone, and where is it written that God doesn't appreciate a little humor?"

"I'm sure He does. Tell me, do you honestly think there were teenagers, like what we have now, in Biblical times?"

"Probably not, especially in the occupied land of Israel. It's probably why there isn't much humor in the Bible. To be factual, the word teenager wasn't used until the thirties after child labor was outlawed and kids were free to grow up a little slower. The kids took complete advantage of this and souped-up their jalopies, put on some swing, and had a lot of fun."

"Is that true, or are you being flip with me? I'm beginning to think you are a bit of a troublemaker."

"I used a modern term for the young adult Jesus. Why is that so scandalous?"

"Okay, so let's get serious. I mean, what made you think of doing a painting of a teenage Jesus?"

"It came to me out of the blue. I was thinking about my son one day, lamenting how for so many years what a close-knit little family we were. Then he turned thirteen and off he went on his own trip. Mom and Dad fell to second or third place, while friends, girlfriends, cars, and parties took center stage. It hit me, it's just like the story of Jesus."

"How is your son like Jesus?"

"No, the life of Jesus and just about everyone else, and how our lives seem to parallel the story in the Bible about Jesus. All we know about him is from his birth in Bethlehem and the three wise men to around twelve when he was preaching in the Temple. Then the missing years showed up, from thirteen to thirty. Where did he go and what was he doing? You hear all kinds of different theories, and they're all fiction."

"That is odd. I've never thought about that," muses Robyn.

"What's interesting is how many people have never thought about the missing years either. It's like some weird mass hypnosis."

"But it is sort of anti-Christian, isn't it? What kind of message do you think a shaved head teenage Jesus sends to kids?"

"Nobody cared that he was painted for centuries as a white guy with blond hair and blue eyes. I simply made him a modern figure; a young man of the times."

"What about the girl with her boob half-exposed?"

"Oh, Mary Magdalene, who according to the Christian faith was a prostitute, although now they admit they might have been wrong about her. Back to your question, her breast represents sexuality—which married people engage in."

"But Jesus wasn't married," snaps Robyn.

"I believe he was," I reply. "The gospels tell us that Mary Magdalene visited his body after the Crucifixion to wash and anoint his body. But women weren't allowed to wash male bodies in Hebrew culture. Only males performed that task—unless you were the man's wife. Clearly, Mary Magdalene was his wife. It tells us so in the Bible. I did do a little research before I started the painting."

I look around the gallery at the large crowd enjoying themselves, and I wish I wasn't stuck with this reporter having to answer Bible questions. And I'm guessing by her flushed cheeks that Robyn is wishing she was interviewing someone else too.

"I painted this as an homage to my son, simple as that. But I can tell you one thing my son and Jesus share."

"What is that?" asks Robyn.

I discovered after I finished the painting, that my son and Jesus share the same birthday."

Robyn smiles, "December twenty-fifth? A Christmas baby!"

"It turns out Jesus was an Easter baby. April seventeenth just like my son, and according to astronomers who have gone back into the history of the universe, a bright star did appear over Israel in the year six AD."

"Oh, my goodness? Do many people know this? One more question, David. I'd like a tagline for the article. In a single sentence, what is the message you would like the viewer to learn from your paintings?"

I find the tagline a tough concept. Who came up with this anyway? How does one describe a work of art in just a few words, when the artist has spent more than a year creating it?

"I don't have a tagline. Isn't that your job as a journalist?"

"Oh, come on now David, don't be difficult."

"I'm ignoring my advice, but how about this: If it pops into my head and it sounds like it might be a good painting I do it. I really can't help it if anyone's offended."

A young woman wearing a hooded sweatshirt pushes her way past Robyn without a warning and ends up standing less than two feet away from me staring into my eyes. I flinch—here it comes, the assassin from Reverend Crantson's hit squad. When she pulls a small dark object from her sweatshirt pocket, I'm immediately reminded of the old black and white video in the Dallas Police Department basement with Lee Harvey Oswald taking a shot to the stomach.

"Can I get a picture of you in front of the painting?" she asks.

"I'm doing an article for my school paper."

Thank God her weapon is only a small, digital camera—I might just make it through tonight's event after all. She wastes no time snapping the picture and quickly disappears into the crowd.

"My, that was rude!" barks Robyn at the backside of the departing girl.

"Well, that should be an informative article," I laugh. "Have you got enough?"

"Oh yes, I almost forgot, I need a picture too. Could you stand next to the painting and smile?" Robyn pulls a stylish smartphone from her leather shoulder bag and takes a quick snapshot.

After I give Robyn my business card in case she has any follow-up questions, I end up leaning on the railing overlooking the gallery. I spot Sidney, and she looks up at me with a big smile, holding two glasses of white wine. She motions for me to join her. Before I do, I study Jesus, The Teenage Years once more. I'm still surprised how many people have never thought about Jesus as a teenager or his missing years, and until the idea came to me a year ago, neither had I. The tattoo has upset a few people who swear Jesus would never allow himself to have a tattoo, but that's Old Testament stuff. Why get hung up on some ancient writings about tattoos, wearing clothing made of more than one kind of cloth, or being put to death for cursing your mother or father?

My eyes turn to a group of young women crowding in close to the painting, giggling as they check out Jesus' six-pack abs, and I have to laugh at how times have changed.

They notice the crowd on the stairway parts as Carla pushes her way through. When she gets to me, she buries her head into my chest and hugs me tightly. I have no idea what the hell is going on, or why she's embracing me.

"What's up, Carla?"

"I just got a call from the museum. The director came over earlier today and checked out your work."

I'm stunned and also concerned; did she like them, or did she give Carla a thumbs down?

"What did she say?" I ask.

Carla takes a deep breath, then offers me a wide smile, and exclaims, "You're in, buddy! I told you I could get you a show, didn't I? And don't forget to thank Teenage Jesus over there, he put you over the top. Get your shit together, David. Art critics and curators can make your hostile, evangelical letter writers seem like angels."

"But if the watchman sees the sword coming and does not blow the trumpet, and the people are not warned, and the sword comes and takes any person from among them, he is taken away in his iniquity; but his blood I will require at the watchman's hand."

–Ezekiel 33:6

THE SWORDSMAN

Holly Quinn finds herself hiding in the dark alcove of a retail store staring at an art gallery wishing those still inside would find another place to go to. The moochers are taking full advantage of the generous pouring of free wine that has kept them here late into the night. When they finally congregate out on the sidewalk, she hears them making plans for another venue where there might be something of interest, or as Holly thinks, more free wine and appetizers.

"What a bunch of bottom-feeders," she mumbles. "How many of these people have ever even bought a painting?"

Holly isn't used to filthy city life. Although she's in excellent physical condition, hiding in the dark for hours has grown a bit tiresome and very boring. She is a willing soldier in the war against the enemies of God, led by her spiritual leader, Reverend Eugene Cranston, but a lack of patience has always been one of her greatest weaknesses.

Holly is rewarded when the street and sidewalk empties of traffic and people and the gallery workers begin scurrying about picking up paper plates, and plastic wine glasses, sweeping and mopping the hardwood floors, and eventually gathering on the sidewalk. The last person out of the gallery is a heavyset, bearded, beatnik type, probably the owner, who takes a proud look at the art-filled gallery and locks up the front doors. Holly hears him thanking his workers for a job well done and winces in anger when one of the workers gushes about one of the artists and his Teenage Jesus painting.

At last! Holly races to the alley in the back of the gallery and lays her backpack on the ground. She kneels and prays, "Dear Heavenly Father, I am your servant and give myself body and soul to the Kingdom of Heaven. I will obey your every word, and only ask that you give me the strength and courage to perform my assigned task."

Holly takes a look down the street to make sure she's alone and runs back to the alley. She stops at the small bathroom window she unlocked earlier in the evening and hopes it's still open. It is, and she lifts it and pushes her pack through. Next, she pulls herself up, squeezing through the opening, and steps gingerly on the toilet lid located below the window. Her foot slips on the damp toilet seat cover and she complains "Gross! That better be Lysol."

Once she's made it upstairs, Holly creeps over to the Teenage Jesus painting, lays her pack down, and pulls out a can of spray paint. She shakes it vigorously and tests it once with a short blast in the air before moving in close to the painting and spraying the word "Heresy" across the lower half of the canvas in bright red paint. She takes a deep satisfying breath, and steps back to admire her work before boasting, "Now, that's what I call art!"

With her assignment complete, Holly pulls a small crowbar out of her pack and races down the stairs to the main entrance.

"See you later sinner!" She shouts before slamming her crowbar into the front door and sending glass exploding onto the sidewalk. The loud alarm begins ringing as Holly slips through the broken glass door and races away, slowing her pace only when she's certain the cops haven't yet responded to the alarm.

Four blocks later, she's standing in front of her small apartment on a dark, dead-end street. As quietly as possible, she slips the key into the lock and opens the door. Safely inside Holly falls against the wall and takes in a deep breath—the first relaxed intake of air she's managed since climbing through the gallery's bathroom window thirty minutes ago. Pink and blue neon lights from a motel across the street dance across a color print of the Teenage Jesus painting tacked up on the wall, only making the art creepier. She stares at it for at least five minutes, thinking about her own party-girl life before turning on a small table lamp and closing the curtain.

"I could use a drink," she jokes to herself.

She knows she can't have a drink. One little drink will send her spiraling back to drugs and one-night stands with guys she would have been disgusted by had she been sober. After a couple of years of alcoholism, Reverend Cranston found her and offered a helping hand with a healthy dose of the Bible, drug rehabilitation, and a healthy diet which brought her back to life.

As a Swordsman for Reverend Cranston, Holly travels light in the reverend's mission to rid America of vile, vulgar, and indecent human behavior. The End of Days draws near, and God willing, they might be able to save a few sinners from eternal damnation. Holly looks at the few, second-hand store articles of clothing hanging in an open closet, then to a framed photograph of her mother as a young woman on the night table next to the bed. When this photo was taken, Holly's mother worked for the local board of education and made a good living. Mother's salary provided Holly with a nice house, fashionable clothes, and a new car, even though mom was a single parent. The money and freedom also allowed her mother a happy hour cocktail or two with her friends from work, then steady drinking at home, which eventually turned into alcoholism.

Holly reminds herself with a prayer before falling asleep that she has the strength not to fall as her mother did. Everyone who looks at the photo remarks how much she resembles her mom— almost like twins, she's been told. The similarities don't stop with their facial features either. Holly knows she is an alcoholic. After a few wild years of high school drinking and running with the A-list jocks, someone forgot to remind her that the party was over. One month after high school graduation her mom committed suicide, and that's when Holly's life began to spiral out of control. The pretty and popular cheerleader who was also the star of the archery team, found herself heading south as a part-time alcoholic junior college student with no job skills. Exhausted from the evening's adventure, Holly collapses on the floral patterned bedspread and falls asleep fully clothed.

Ten hours later, a dancing beam of light travels across the bedroom wall through an opening in the curtain and hits a sleeping Holly square in the face. She groans and turns over, but she knows she's not going back to sleep, thank you Mister Sunbeam. Holly rolls onto her back, yawns, and lazily stretches her arms over her head. When she turns to the side, she's greeted by the wise-ass smirk of Teenage Jesus and that girl with the painted face who isn't even attempting to cover up her slightly exposed breast even though they're walking through a crowded town square.

This time, Holly doesn't look away from the painting like she normally does. It makes her think about the difficulties she experienced growing up with an alcoholic mother, and a father who died tragically when she was only ten. She thinks about the Bible story of Bethlehem and the Virgin Mary, pregnant and unwed until Joseph married her. Their baby was born in a barn because they were so poor. The evil King Herod had been told by the Three Wise Men that a new king had been born. The news shocked the King, who now wanted him dead because he was afraid Jesus would take over his throne. He searched everywhere for Jesus, but couldn't find him until one of his soldiers heard of a baby in Bethlehem who everyone said was the Son of God. King Herod sent his soldiers to Bethlehem and told his soldiers to kill all the baby boys under two years old, hoping the one trumpeted as the new king would be one of them and he could keep his power.

Holly doesn't know if all of that is true, but her mother told her this story often, to remind Holly of how difficult and dangerous the world is, especially for a young woman. But mostly, the story made her sad, and to this day, she can't stand to listen to the Christmas carol, Oh, Little Town of Bethlehem.

*A star shone in heaven beyond all the other stars,
and its light was inexpressible, and its novelty struck terror
into men's minds. All the rest of the stars, together with the
sun and moon were the chorus to this star; but that sent
out its light exceedingly above them all. And men began to
be troubled to think whence this new star came so unlike all
the others. Hence all the power of magic became dissolved;
men's ignorance was taken away; and the old kingdom was
abolished; God himself appeared in the form of a man, for the
renewal of eternal life.*

OH, LITTLE TOWN OF BETHLEHEM

Three elegantly dressed men from Persia draw their richly embroidered silk robes about them and leave the small barn, as that is what it was called when they inquired at the inn, but to their eyes, looks more like a cave. The enchanting spell was broken when the husband of the young mother asked all to leave so that his wife might finally rest. The men had traveled for months following the brightest star ever seen in their time, a sign that they believed foretold the miraculous birth of a new king who might be the son of God.

The child's father, a man named Joseph, explained to the Persian men how they had traveled for many days to reach the village of Bethlehem, a journey so exhausting for his wife Mary, that he had feared losing the child along the way. Joseph complained to the Persian men that he had given up many lucrative building contracts to travel to the little town, forced by Caesar's census to count every man, woman, and child to collect taxes to support his massive army. Citizens were obligated to travel to the place of their birth, and like Joseph, most lived elsewhere.

Arriving in Bethlehem, they discovered no lodging to be found. Every inn and spare room, of which there were very few to begin with, were filled. Some did offer to give up their beds to the pregnant girl, but guided by heavenly voices only she could hear, she refused and opted for a quiet barn on the outskirts of town.

The Persian men take a last glance at the child peacefully asleep, wrapped in a fine cloth, and held under the watchful eye of his young mother. Gathering outside the barn, they are met by the Elder of Bethlehem, a man named Eron.

"Was your journey in vain," asks Eron, "or is the child the divine one?"

"Who decides what is truth? But something remarkable has occurred, of that, we can be certain," remarks Balthazar.

The three men turn toward the desert and the land far to the East where they began their journey almost three months earlier. Melchior looks toward the hazy glow of human activity emanating from Jerusalem in the distance with the golden dome of the Temple casting its presence even in the darkness.

"This is a land of cunning and robberies. What chance does a child stand in this cruel place?" muses Melchior.

"Truth walks through the world unharmed," replies Balthazar. "The child will be safe. Of that I am certain."

"We have seen him!" cries Melchior. "Balthazar, we blundered in telling Herod of our journey."

Balthazar furrows his brow. "We were naive in thinking that the builder of a Great Temple to himself would welcome a Messiah. We cannot return to him with news of the child's whereabouts. The man is cruel and wicked and he would make certain none challenge his power. Gaspar, what is your view?"

Gaspar replies, "I do not trust that black-haired devil. He will bow to no child."

"It is agreed then. We shall return by way of another route, and make no mention to anyone of our witness," says Balthazar.

Gaspar confidently boasts, "I do not fear Herod's reach as he rules only in the West. The wind will erase any evidence of our footprints and we shall return by any route we choose."

"We must warn the young father," says Melchior.

"I will tell him of your fears," replies Eron. "We will protect the child at any cost."

"At any cost?" wonders Melchior. "I suggest that once the mother and child can travel, they flee this land as quickly as possible."

"If you have told Herod of the child's birth," says Eron, "it will not be long before his spies discover his whereabouts."

Two dignified men lounge on comfortable, plush chairs in the elegantly furnished salon of Herod's palace, separated by a wood and finely detailed mosaic-tiled table. Attendants stand nearby in wait, in case the king demands immediate attention. Tonight Herod has summoned his astrologer, Uzziel, a scholar held in high esteem in the palace, as he is the only man allowed to speak absolute truth to the king without fear of punishment, which is usually a most brutal death. For weeks the concerned old king has been worried when a bright star, brighter than any ever seen before, appeared above the skies over Jerusalem.

King Herod sits back in his chair fiddling with his long black hair and beard as Uzziel, his eyes turned white by cataracts and is nearly blind, runs his hands over a small pile of gold coins.

"What do the coins tell you, old Uzziel?" asks Herod. "What of that king those Persians sought? Guided to our land by a bright star; what nonsense!"

"Oh, mighty Herod, today they tell us a great story. On this day in our land, he is born."

Herod perks to attention and slams his fist down hard on the table. The commotion startles the nearby attendants who race to the table to kneel and bow obsequiously before him. Herod brusquely waves them off and shouts, "What madness is this? None shall cast a shadow on my glory! Tell me his whereabouts, and I shall destroy this impostor!"

Uzziel slowly collects his coins, as it is not often he can enjoy the king's discomfort. His position in the palace keeps him safe from harm, but his secret kept well hidden from all is his complete disdain for the old king.

"Exaltation and magic envelop the child. You will not be able to harm him," smiles Uzziel, as he stacks the coins into a neat pile.

Herod's thick dark eyebrows twitch, and his painted lips quiver uncontrollably. He nervously runs his hands through his beard to calm himself, then leans into Uzziel with a most wicked, ugly grin.

"I must see this newborn king for myself. If you speak the truth, then I will kneel at his feet and worship him. Tell me, how shall I find his highness?"

"He is in a long, fertile valley. I see soft grazing lands. Fresh water streams sparkle in the sunlight, and a small village rests on a rocky plateau."

※ ※ ※

"Arise, Mary! Quickly now!" whispers Joseph. "We must leave at once. Herod's soldiers are coming to take away our child. Hurry while it is still dark. I have packed our belongings."

Mary wipes away the sleep from her eyes and asks, "What of the villagers? If the soldiers do not find our child, they might harm others. You must warn them!"

"This has already been done, wife," answers Joseph. "I have informed Elder Eron. He is aware of their approach."

"Then, they must leave while it is still safe."

"They will not leave, even as I pleaded with them to do so," replies Joseph. "The Elders and families have decided that our child must be protected at all costs."

"Certainly one of them will tell the soldiers of our flight."

"Dearest wife, Mary," says Joseph softly, "the good people of Bethlehem know it is not only this family chosen by the Father. They will protect us, and the Lord will protect them."

The small village of Bethlehem sits high on a rocky ridge overlooking a fertile valley filled with fields of grass, neatly tended orchards, and vineyards. The waning crescent moon barely illuminates a cluster of darkened stone homes surrounding a town square surrounding an ancient, twisted olive tree. Most in the village are asleep as two shadowy figures race silently through the town, dipping their brushes in a bucket of sheep's blood, then splashing a large "X" on a dozen or more wooden doors.

One villager is not sleeping. A young, single mother named Elizabeth sits by her sleeping child in a room lit by an oil lamp. She sings a soothing melody while softly rocking in her chair but her song ends abruptly when she begins crying, making it impossible to continue. She drops her head into her hands looks lovingly at her child and repeats over and over in a whisper, "God has chosen us, Matthew...God has chosen us. Blessed are those who walk with God." She kisses him on the forehead and takes a last sad look at him before snuffing out the lamp and lying down on her bed.

A sleeping dog's quiet growling outside compels her to creep cautiously to a small window for a peek through the curtain. She waits for her eyes to adjust to the darkness and searches for the danger that is sure to be coming soon. She sees nothing out of the ordinary and returns to her bed.

Bethlehem's watchdog is sleeping against the cool of a brick wall, stirring uncomfortably as if having a bad dream. Though he appears to be sleeping, his ears are constantly turning and twitching, searching for any unfamiliar or threatening sounds. *"Something is wrong,"* a voice growls within. Maybe it's a light wind rattling the leaves, or the chirping of crickets might be all it is, but instinct tells him otherwise. *"Wake up!"* the voice within calls to him. He knows his responsibility, the same as his forefathers which is to protect the villagers sleeping in their homes. He takes a lazy stretch and stands up to peer over the low stone wall to the valley below. He waits patiently with his eyes darting to and fro, searching for the slightest movement. Without much light from the weak moon, he's unable to spot anything out of the ordinary. He stands up on the wall and sniffs the air, and there it is—he can smell it and it's not a familiar scent.

The crickets suddenly stop chirping, which is another signal he knows not to ignore. The strange odors that travel on the slight breeze now fill his nose, and along with his remarkable hearing, he picks up the sound of a twig cracking not too far in the distance. Finally, he spots them—men, many of them moving silently through the recently cut wheat fields heading toward the village. He stretches his neck for a better look just to be certain there is genuine cause for alarm. The thought of another beating from his enraged master roused from sleep because of a false warning, forces him to hesitate for a second. The strangers are now at the head of the trail leading to the village gate. *"Certainly a warning is needed,"* he tells himself. But it's already too late. Before he can bark out a warning. An arrow traveling invisibly through the night slams into his chest and knocks him off his feet. He feels no pain, certainly not as painful as the abscess caused by a burr that burrowed deep into his skin, but he knows he has failed in his task. He barely manages a weak, quiet yelp before hitting the ground, dead.

A dozen well-armed soldiers enter the square and stand in formation at attention. The captain with his entourage of junior officers is the last to enter and quietly direct the troops to action, pointing out locations of doors marked with a painted red X. The soldiers move through the streets lighting lanterns and assuming positions in front of each marked door.

A young soldier, almost a child himself, raises a horn to his lips and blows loud, the signal for the soldiers to begin kicking in doors and rushing into the dark homes of the sleeping villagers. The quiet night is interrupted by terrified screams echoing throughout the town. The few townsfolk who block their front doors in an attempt to slow the soldiers' progress are easily shoved or knocked to the ground. Once inside, tables and chairs are kicked aside in a mad search for young boys. The mayhem wakes the children and their cries and whimpering make them easy prey and are roughly yanked from their beds and carried outside.

Elizabeth is also dragged out of her small home. She wrestles with a soldier fighting to keep Matthew from being ripped from her arms until the child is taken away forcefully by another soldier who shoves Elizabeth to the ground. She makes a desperate grab for her child and screams his name before falling face down onto the cobblestone street. Although she is weeping uncontrollably, she wraps the her hand around a cobblestone and recalls watching her baby, Matthew as he learned to crawl, laughing as he slowly and cautiously climbed over each stone. Only recently he had begun stepping over them gingerly while walking upright. How he laughed with her, proud of his accomplishment and she had looked forward to the day when he would be running over the cobblestones with other boys and girls, racing through the village and playfully challenging the other children to see who would be the fastest runner.

The soldiers emerge from many other houses holding wailing small boys. Elizabeth rises from the street, then turns to her fellow citizens and screams, "Where is he? Where is our God? Why does he not come to our aid as promised?"

Most of Bethlehem's mothers and fathers are not fighting for their loved ones as she is. They stand by with their heads bowed chanting silently, He will come, hoping for the miracle.

A soldier delivers the captain the first child, Matthew. The soldier unwraps the blanket and tosses it to the ground. He rudely holds a squealing Matthew by a leg, upside down as one would do when buying a hen at the market, and waits for his orders. The captain takes a glance at Matthew's small penis and nods affirmatively.

The soldier takes a deep breath and grimaces as he quickly slices his knife across Matthew's chubby throat and is sprayed with the child's blood.

The shock silences the townspeople and soldiers alike until Elizabeth breaks the quiet when she screams, "No! Not my son! Dear God ... please!"

Elizabeth crawls on her hands and knees to her bleeding child and jumps to her feet and begins grappling with the confused soldier for her boy who stupidly looks over to his captain for guidance. The captain waves him off.

"Let her be," he shrugs nonchalantly.

Elizabeth grabs Matthew and races out of the square and ends up squatting next to a building gasping for air attempting to stop her child's bleeding. She rips off a portion of her dress and pinches closed the wound on his neck. The strip of material might stop the bleeding she hopes as she closes her eyes and rocks her child, no longer praying for the miracle promised by the Elders, but only for this nightmare to end and for her son to survive.

The town square has become deathly still. Even the lower-ranking soldiers are shocked into silence by the cruelty of their assigned task. Shockingly or not the captain has his orders. "Where is the child we seek? Produce him now or we shall destroy every boy child until there are none!"

The village elder Eron, steps forward and calmly replies, "The one you seek does not exist. Your king was misled."

"You dare lie to a King's officer? Answer me!"

Eron holds his tongue and is rewarded with a vicious shove to the ground followed by a solid kick to the stomach.

The captain glares at the villagers. "I see plotting. I see foxes, and dogs...liars!"

Kill every young boy until we receive an answer."

One child after another suffers the knife, and the mothers and fathers stand silently with their fists clenched and heads bowed, praying for God to end this madness. Each death is followed by an unearthly howl echoing through the town, but it's not coming from the mothers or fathers of the village, it's the scream of a mother squatting in an alley holding her bleeding son. God is not coming on this night.

JOY TO THE WORLD

Rows of dormant pistachio trees strung with thousands of white Christmas lights illuminate the way for dozens of partygoers making their way up a brick walkway that leads to the front door of Mark and Christine's modern, Tuscan-style home. Once described in a magazine article as *California Dreamin'*, it looks and feels more like a modern Roman villa. The home sits high on a ridge overlooking acres of vineyards and hundreds of olive trees planted in neat rows that command a spectacular view of the valley and the shimmering waters of the Pacific Ocean beyond.

A large picture window frames a heavily decorated, twelve-foot-tall Christmas tree strategically placed to overlook the valley. When the guests arrive in the cobblestone courtyard, they enter the house through oversized double wooden doors into a spacious two-story foyer. There, they are greeted by Joy to the World being played on a baby grand piano by a very competent pianist. Moving about the room, young servers in starched white long-sleeve shirts and black slacks, offer champagne in stemmed glassware with Mark and Christine's names etched into them.

Many of the guests take a cursory glance at a painting titled, *Jesus, The Teenage Years* that dominates the foyer before continuing to the party except for two teenage girls who stop and study it.

"He is so freaking hot!" remarks one of the girls.

Her companion leans into the painting and places a kiss on

the protective glass and moans, "I love Teenage Jesus!"

"I'd do him!" exclaims her friend.

"You can't do Jesus!" replies her shocked friend.

"Humph," remarks an offended guest who turns up her nose at the girls and quickly walks away.

The girls cover their mouths and giggle before running into the ballroom-sized living room where the Christmas party is in full swing. Servers glide smoothly about the room with platters of appetizers like Chinese coconut shrimp balls, apricots stuffed with herbs and cheese, crackers with curried lamb, or crackers smeared with something creamy and pink.

On the stairway, a half-dozen teenage girls holding a velvet-covered songbook accompany the pianist, quietly humming *Joy to the World*.

Christine walks over to the pianist and the girls and signals them to quiet. She turns and smiles at her guests and taps on her wine glass with a fork. Most quieted down immediately except for a few guests so engaged in conversation and completely oblivious to the sudden drop in the noise level.

Christine taps her glass once more, this time a little louder. "May I have everyone's attention, please? First off, I would like to thank all of you so much for joining us tonight. I know it's difficult braving the warm Christmas weather in California, so we're very happy you could all make it! Tonight, we have a special treat in store for you. The girls have been working on Christmas carols all week, and if I do say so myself, they are sounding mighty professional."

Christine sweeps her hand across the choir like a conductor, "Take it away, girls!" A pretty blonde girl steps in front of the choral group hums the key, and then counts, "One, two, three!"

The girls begin singing, *Little Saint Nick*, a bouncy holiday tune by the Beach Boys:

Well, way up north where the air gets cold,

There's a tale about Christmas that you've all been told, And a
real famous cat all dressed up in red

And he spends the whole year workin' in his sled...

The party guests join in the chorus section and begin singing, some actually on key:

... It's the little Saint Nick

Ooh, the little Saint Nick

It's the little Saint Nick

Yeah, little Saint Nick.

The song ends with everyone singing, "ooh, ooh, ooh, Merry Christmas Baby," repeated at least a dozen times until the song stumbles to an end with inebriated laughter and loud boisterous applause.

I grab a drink from one of the servers when a jazzy version of Jingle Bells sends me out of the room into the foyer, and I end up standing in front of my Teenage Jesus painting. A few moments later, Mark and his daughter Mimi leave the noisy ballroom and join me.

Mark asks, "David, what do you think of your painting under glass and the new exquisite frame?"

"It's spectacular. I think I might have been able to get more for it."

"Nah," laughs Mark, "it's the frame that makes it look expensive. But I'm glad you demanded I keep the spray-painted "Heresy" on it. It gives it a wicked edge."

"David, all my friends love him," says Mimi enthusiastically. "We all wonder what he was really like."

"No one will ever know, Mimi," I reply. "The guys who wrote the Bible must have thought he wasn't doing anything important when he was a teenager or they would have included it in the Bible, don't you think?"

"Just another crabby, suicidal teenager," laughs Mimi.

"I think he was a troubled child prodigy who crapped out in his teenage years. Look at Van Cliburn who was also a child prodigy before disappearing when he was thirteen after a brilliant career. Then, he came back when he was thirty, just like Jesus."

"Who's Van Cliburn?" asks Mimi.

I have to laugh, and I'm showing my age. "He was a great classical pianist about forty years ago, Mimi."

Mark adds, "He was a genius on the piano at the age of eight! I believe it was the babies that were killed in Bethlehem that has something to do with Jesus disappearing."

"The what?" gasps Mimi.

"The children of Bethlehem," replies Mark. "They were killed because of the birth of Jesus."

The choir of Mimi's college girlfriends enters the foyer and the noise level rises to a deafening level of chatter, laughter, and joking. One of the girls grabs Mimi's arm and tugs her away from us. "Come on, Mimi!" she laughs. "We're gonna hit the streets, babe! Get your coat on because the temperature might drop into the mid-sixties!"

"Thanks Kristy, but I want to hang out with the folks tonight. Sorry girls," replies Mimi.

"Awe, come on, Mimi!" chime in the other girls.

"We won't stay out late," pleads Kristy. "It'll be fun! We'll get some cute guys to sing with us. It'll be a blast!

Another girl takes Mimi's hand, leans in close and tells her in a soft, flirty voice, "We can crash all kinds of parties singing carols."

"Not tonight guys, I'm happy right here," says Mimi.

"Okay for you," shrugs Kristy, then tells Mark, "Thanks for the great party!"

The girls head to the door, giggling and laughing, over what, I have no idea. Each girl kisses Mimi on the cheek and a quick hug as they leave.

"You guys have fun!" she calls out. "See you later!"

The girls make their way down the long pathway to the parking area singing Walking in a Winter Wonderland, and with their car windows open on this warm night, we can hear their singing echoing through the valley even after they've traveled far down the road.

Mimi slowly closes the door and walks back to us looking serious, and very deep in thought. Mark gives her a big hug and says, "You should have gone, kiddo. You deserve a little fun after surviving a bloody revolution."

"After what revolution?" I ask.

"You didn't know?" replies Mark. "Certainly we've told you."

"This is the first I've heard about it. I thought she was studying Spanish in Mexico or South America."

""Well, sort of. Mimi got trapped in Guatemala while working on her degree in Central American indigenous people and modern-day Mayans."

"Come on, dad. Don't bore David."

"This doesn't sound like it's going to be boring at all. I'm interested; what the hell happened?" I ask.

Mimi looks at the floor and sighs as if she would rather not be reminded. "I was helping nuns run a women's health clinic in a

Mayan village when private security forces showed up and started shooting. It was supposed to be a safe area after the civil war they had twenty years ago had been settled."

"Why were they attacking the Mayans?"

"It was a union struggle, with the workers being mostly Mayans. The hired goons from the coffee growers attacked them after a few union reps arrived to help them organize. The growers complained to the government that they were communists, and the corrupt government turned a blind eye to it after receiving bribes from the growers."

"What happened? I mean, how did you get out of there?"

"They attacked the workers out in the fields first, who fortunately carried automatic weapons given to them years ago by the *Sandinistas*. While the fighting was going on, the village leader ordered us to follow him into the jungle where we hid out for close to a week before things calmed down."

"How did you get out of the country?"

"When the Catholic nuns came in to care for the wounded, the villagers insisted we leave with them when all the victims were taken care of. I even got to help which was the best thing I've ever done." Mimi grows reflective for a moment then continues, "I didn't want to abandon the village—they're so brave, but they didn't want me to get hurt. I plan on going back someday."

"Well, we're just happy she made it out safely and she's here with us. So, Merry Christmas!" exclaims Mark.

"God bless the baby Jesus," I say as we clink our glasses,

Mimi laughs and chimes in, "Yeah! Let's not let my story make us all gloomy, and speaking of gloomy, is it true what you said Dad, that babies were killed because of Jesus?"

"Absolutely. Some say that as many as two dozen were killed."

"That's so horrible! Why?"

"That's a good question," responds Mark. "Why would God allow it to happen to his own son and His chosen people?"

"You know Mark," I comment. "The Catholic church doesn't promote that story anymore. If you've read the Bible, only the Gospel of Matthew even mentions the birth of Jesus."

I wonder "Why am I defending the church?" But I see that Mark is just warming up to the subject at hand.

"Since we bought the painting, I've been doing a fair amount of research about his missing years, David. So, I have read the Bible, and many other non-canonical writings."

"I hope I'm not responsible for turning you into a theology student," I laugh. "I've always wondered though; if the angel came to Joseph in a dream telling him of Herod's arrival, why didn't he tell the rest of the village?"

"Yes!" replies Mark. "Why didn't he? We don't know when the angel came, but let's say it was in time to warn the others. If Joseph told them, why didn't they flee? They must have known Herod was looking for the infant and would go to great lengths to find him. Torture was pretty commonplace back then."

Mimi adds in a flat voice, "Maybe the people of Bethlehem felt they were chosen too. They were the first Christian martyrs."

"Way to go, Mimi! A very interesting approach—they were chosen, just like Jesus. What do you think, David?"

"First, there weren't any Christians yet, Mimi, but it would make them martyrs. Then, later on in life, the twelve-year-old Jesus found out about this killing and turned into an angry, rebellious young man. I know I would have if that happened to me. It's probably why we don't know anything about his missing years."

"Why did you give Jesus a tattoo? Was it to emphasize his

rebellious, delinquent side?" asks Mimi.

"Yep. That tattoo has got me into a lot of trouble with Bible-thumpers. I riled up a whole nest of nut cases when my exhibit got picked up on the internet. Man, those people are so uptight—no sense of humor!"

"Is that why poor Teenage Jesus got tagged?" asks Mimi.

"Absolutely. I know the radical Jesus freaks will hate me for saying this, but with the vandalism and the following publicity, the painting has taken on a life of its own far beyond my part in it. It's evolving."

Mark laughs. "That's pretty funny, seeing as they don't believe in evolution."

"They're not supposed to believe in revenge either, but look at all the Planned Parenthood bombings."

"No one would hurt you, David," says Mimi. "All my friends love Teenage Jesus, especially my girlfriends."

"That's sweet, Mimi," I reply. "But I'm not too worried, I have protection—a very serious guardian angel."

"When did you get religious and start believing in angels?" asks Mark.

"You don't have to be religious to believe in angels. Anyway, mine is more like an avenging angel. People have gotten into big trouble trying to screw me over."

Mark laughs, "You're insane."

"I'm not kidding. Go ask Sidney."

"David, did you notice the lipstick marks on Teenage Jesus?" says Mimi. "All my girlfriends kiss him for good luck."

"I have," I reply. "I don't know who's the bigger sinner, me or you guys."

Mimi's cell phone begins to chime and she sits down on the

stairway, puts the phone to her ear and sighs. "What's up, Evan?"

Mimi can tell Evan's been drinking. His tongue is thick and his speech is sloppy as he slurs, "Hey Mimi, it's Christmas, you should be here!"

Mimi takes a deep breath to calm herself. "It sounds like fun, but I want to hang out with my folks. I never see them anymore!"

"Oh, I see how it is," replies Evan, "you got some old hot guy to dance with, huh?"

Mimi stares at the phone for a few seconds, then continues with Evan. "Let's talk about this later, okay? You're welcome to come over and hang out...when you sober up."

"I'm not fuckin' drunk! And, I'm not gonna to leave this kick-ass party to have cocktails on the veranda with Mom and Dad and the senior set!"

"I'm hanging up now, Evan."

"Shit, I'm sorry, Mimi. It's just that I miss you so much. You know that don't you?"

"Yes, Evan, I know. I'll call you soon, okay? Good night."

"Oh yeah, you'll call me," sneers Evan, and abruptly hangs up.

Mimi quietly curses, "Asshole." She places her cell phone into her purse and wraps her arms around her knees, lost in thought and on the verge of tears.

"Has anyone seen my husband?" yells Christine above the noise of the party.,

After Mark ran off to look after his wife and his guests, I notice Mimi sitting on the stairs, and it looks like she's ready to burst into tears. "Do you mind if I join you?" I ask. "If you want to be alone I understand, but you look kind of upset."

"You might say that," she sniffles. "Thanks for asking. I could use a little advice."

41

"What's going on?" I ask. "Christmas is supposed to be a happy time and you don't look too cheerful."

"I'm okay," replies Mimi. "It's my ex-boyfriend Evan. We broke up and he can't figure out how to get over me," and then laughs through the tears and says, "Oh my God, that sounded so conceited, didn't it? Anyway, Evan used to be the coolest guy. He was sweet and loving, but then he started drinking. I begged him to stop, but it always ended up with us fighting. Finally, I got tired of arguing with him about his drinking and left him."

"Has he admitted to you or anyone that he has an alcohol problem?" I ask.

"No! Whenever I ask him to get help, he tells me to mind my own business. If I ask him if he's been drinking, he denies it and gets defensive, followed by blubbering apologies about how much he loves me."

"I'm sorry to hear that, although it sounds kind of typical these days. A lot of people don't handle rejection very well. You should be careful, a situation like this can become abusive and develop into dangerous behavior. It's too bad; I always liked Evan."

"He liked you too. He can be charming and funny, but his drinking has gotten pretty old, along with his bad behavior. What about you, David? Did you ever have a high school sweetheart you couldn't get over?"

"Well... sort of. I had a group of girls who I hung out with. None of us were serious about a relationship, we just wanted to have fun, although we'd date each other. I had one serious relationship that ended up being a bit of a heartbreaker. When we broke up, I was a mess, especially because it came out of the blue. One moment we were having fun, and the next moment, she broke up with me. It was confusing for a seventeen-year-old. I think she realized that going steady with a surf bum might be a dead end." Mimi laughs, "She might have at least talked to you about her concerns."

"That might have helped, but I would have remained a surf bum, regardless. Still, I was crushed."

"It looks like you survived."

I nod in agreement. "Fortunately, I found Sidney."

"I'm glad you did, especially Sidney. She is the coolest woman I've ever known. Plus, she's really beautiful."

"I couldn't agree with you more."

"Let's forget about Evan," says Mimi. "I've been wanting to ask you about Teenage Jesus over there. What I like about him is how you were able to capture that attitude of being a young adult—so full of yourself and so insecure at the same time."

"I'm glad you think so. I was worried that I had become too old to remember what being young was like."

"Not you," laughs Mimi. "You nailed it. It's that time in your life when emotions dictate everything. You know, that period when we find ourselves physically adult, but emotionally immature and confused about the future. Plus, we're still dependent on mom and dad for support. It's a pretty frustrating time."

"And all of that hidden behind an attitude of cool, right?"

Mimi laughs in agreement. "Of course! When are you ever going to be cooler than when you're nineteen? You know, David, I think Teenage Jesus would make a great movie!"

"Oh, I don't think so. Can you imagine a movie called, *Jesus, the Teenage Years*? With a title like that, they'd turn it into a goofy romantic comedy."

"Yeah, I can see it. Jesus and Judas are the best of friends until a hot chick shows up and comes between them."

"That would be Mary Magdalene?" I chuckle.

"It's the perfect formula movie," Mimi says. "They could do a road trip to Bethlehem where the best friend turns out to be a conceited jerk and tries to seduce Mary. She tells Jesus, who then beats the crap out of Judas. In the end, Mary and Jesus ride off into the sunset to seek fame and poverty."

"I see you've given this script some thought."

Mimi laughs, "At least two minutes! Okay, how about *The Missing Years?* That's a pretty serious title. I think Hollywood has filmed the crucifixion often enough—what's wrong with a movie about a young adult Jesus? I think it would make a fortune!"

"Complete with protesters in front of every theater!" I add. "No one would ever film a movie about Jesus that didn't stick to the Biblical narrative."

"You're probably right. I mean, look at how your poor painting got vandalized. I can only imagine hundreds of theaters getting trashed by angry evangelicals."

"That painting was trouble enough let alone a blockbuster movie. The very idea of it gives me the chills—hell, I'd probably get assassinated. Yeech, let's change the subject. How is school going?"

Mimi pauses. "I'm not going back to school this year."

"Really? Why not?"

"I'm tired of wasting mom and dad's money, especially when I don't even know what I want to major in. I'm not going back until I have a clear idea."

"Wow, that's pretty mature of you."

"Thank you. I'm glad there's at least one adult who thinks I'm doing the right thing. I've just landed a decent job working for an attorney who helps battered women. And, I found a cute little apartment close to the beach. So, I'm feeling pretty good about myself these days."

"I've got some prints if you need to fill the walls."

"Okay, count on it. So, tell me about our boy Jesus over there. Why did you make him look like such a stud? I've read that Jesus wasn't all that remarkable looking."

"I don't think anyone knows what he looked like, except, for sure he didn't have blond hair and blue eyes. Historically, Israel was at the center of major trade routes from the east. Romans were building seaports, warehouses, roads, bridges, army barracks, and there were a lot of Roman settlements too—the first tract homes," I laugh. "They would have needed local builders and skilled tradesmen, and I've read that they paid well, too."

"So Jesus and Joseph would have been making decent wages, right?" says Mimi.

"Right. Jesus might have been the son of a successful general contractor. I discovered that his uncle, Joseph of Arimathea, was a wealthy merchant with cargo ships, and with his political influence, they were probably middle-class at least. Think of Joseph and Jesus with a crew of masons and carpenters building lavish villas—it would have made them rich. Who else was going to do it?"

"He was a contractor! Oh my God! He would have been built like a..."

"A brick shit-house! Plus, he was smart. How else was he able to have hundreds of people following him around the countryside later on in his life? A very cool Messiah indeed. But that came later. At nineteen he was a young man with a bad attitude about a corrupt church, the Roman occupation, and even toward his parents for creating the whole myth about his birth."

"And the children killed too," says Mimi.

"Definitely. What about his father, Joseph, who disappears in the Bible story? There are stories that he was crucified too, swept up in a mass arrest after Jewish zealots attacked a Roman settlement. What would that do to your attitude if your father was executed by foreign invaders?"

"Wow," says Mimi. "That's why your painting is so much more than it appears. You've done some research, haven't you?"

"Probably too much," I laugh. "Thank god your dad is doing it now, probably to explain to his clients why he bought my blasphemous painting. At least now I can get on with the rest of my life and paint something else."

THE PHARISEE

News of a painting, *Jesus, The Teenage Years,* surfaced on the Internet and caught the attention of folks who look out for this kind of stuff. Dozens of evangelical ministries throughout the country forwarded the picture to the many religious communities around the country, including that of Reverend Eugene Cranston, spiritual leader at the Hilltop Calvary Church located above the town of Pine Valley, Idaho. The contemptible image makes Reverend Cranston's blood boil, infuriating him so greatly that he had considered calling his physician. He rubs his chest, feeling as if he might be having a heart attack as he stares at the nearly exposed breast of a young harlot walking side-by-side with a delinquent punk depicted as our Lord, Jesus Christ. He gasps for breath and cries out, "Who is this artist? He is no more than the devil's servant!"

Reverend Cranston calls one of his ministers into the office and points to the painting lying on his desk. He hesitates to even touch it, lest he be tainted by sin. "What kind of man would even think about painting our Lord in this manner? Jesus didn't have a shaved head, nor did he have any gang tattoos! And Jesus Christ, our lord, and savior, would never consort with some young harlot with her tit showing!"

The minister nods his head in agreement. "This is of modern society, with its drugs and loose moral behavior, responsible for causing the demise of humanity."

"This is the worst kind of blasphemy!" replies Reverend Cranston angrily.

"Shall we call a special meeting for tomorrow night?" asks the Minister.

Tomorrow night in this remote Idaho location is not a quiet time. A billion crickets sing a non-stop rhythmic mating chant as they accompany the churchgoers of Hilltop Church singing praise to God accompanied by an electric guitar player. They have gathered in the small church, which, unlike the ornate palaces of the Catholic Pope, features no-nonsense furnishings of pale green linoleum flooring and harsh overhead lights. God is not impressed by man's ostentatiousness.

Reverend Cranston stands at the podium waiting patiently until his congregation finishes the song. The followers of Reverend Cranston are serious and pious, and tonight is a strong turnout, as it usually is for these hastily called events. The End of Days is drawing near and there is an important topic to discuss.

Reverend Cranston clears his throat and lifts the color photocopy of the painting, *Jesus, The Teenage Years* in the air for all to see. He waves it over his head and angrily shakes his fist.

"I have here... I have in my hands, the work of one of the worst kinds of sinners! This hideous piece of trash was delivered to me in the mail last week, but you can find it instantly and twenty-four hours a day, on the internet!

The congregation hisses, "BOO!"

"We all know about the inner...net; home of pornography with lustful, disgusting images...and nakedness. It is this exact kind of mockery and rebellion which God's word has some very serious warnings about."

"Blasphemy! Blasphemy!" yells out the congregation before they begin clapping their hands while repeatedly chanting, "Blasphemy! Blasphemy!"

Reverend Cranston holds up his hands and calls for silence before continuing, "I thought I had seen it all! This piece of rubbish and the unrepentant sinner who created it, should not even be remotely linked to our Savior, who, in all his holiness would never ...would never..."

Reverend Cranston shoves the wrinkled photocopy to his chest, falls to his knees, and sobs. The congregation jumps to its feet and shouts, "Tell us, Brother Cranston! Tell us! The congregation jumps to its feet and shouts, "Tell us, Brother Cranston! Tell us!"

Using the podium to pull himself up, Reverend Cranston wipes at his eyes, "He...he would never. I can't even think of words to adequately describe this kind of blasphemy! The seducing spirits have taken hold of this man and he should fall on his face before our holy God and beg forgiveness for changing the meaning of scripture!"

Reverend Cranston lifts his face to the heavens and cries out with his arms reaching skyward. "I beg this servant of Satan for his soul's sake, to renounce this lustful depiction of Christ, and try to arrest the damage already done to unsuspecting teenagers."

The shocked congregation gasps.

"From the beginning, when God spoke to Abraham and said, 'Go forth from your country, and from your relatives and from your father's house, to the land which I will show you; and I will make you a great nation, and I will bless you. And the one who curses you, I will curse."

Two men rise from their front-row seats and help Reverend Cranston take his seat near the podium and return proudly to their chairs. The reverend rests his head in his hands, deep in thought. A skeptic might believe this to be nothing more than a well-rehearsed act. And it is well-rehearsed, but it is no act, at least in the theatrical sense of the word. The reverend is a serious man who strongly believes in the literal interpretation of the Good Book, and that this artist's satanic creation is a poison arrow directed straight into the heart of God's word.

After a moment of reflection, he raises his eyes and shouts out, his words echo throughout the small frame building. "If the Watchman sees the sword coming and does not blow the trumpet, and the people are not warned, and the sword takes any person from among them; his blood I will require! Ezekiel, 33:6!"

Silence descends upon the small room—even the crickets stop their ceaseless racket; as if waiting for the Reverend Cranston to complete his sermon.

"Steps have been taken," he says. "The trumpet has been sounded. The sword shall be broken!"

THE WATCHMAN

Upon waking, a sleep-deprived Holly shakes her head in disgust that she left the television on all night. She pushes herself to a sitting position and fluffs up her two pillows for use as a headboard before reaching for her Bible. The night of art destruction followed by the adrenaline rush kept her awake late into the night and early morning hours. She softly rubs the cool leather cover of the Bible on her face for comfort and prays.

"I have done as you have asked of me, Lord," she whispers. "The sinner has been warned."

Holly looks over to the print of, *Jesus, The Teenage Years* for a few seconds. Maybe it's the lack of sleep or some deeply hidden guilt about defacing the painting, but today it seems it is richer in color than she remembered. Also, the wise-ass smirk on the young man the artist called, Teenage Jesus, doesn't look like a smirk at all. Instead, it now appears to be a welcoming smile. She would never admit to herself that it's an all-knowing smile, but the artist seems to have captured a look that suggests that maybe his subject is a bit more complex than her first impression.

Holly's thoughts are interrupted when her cell phone begins chiming When The Saints Go Marching In. She lays her Bible down, scrambles over the bed to her backpack, unzips the flap, and finds the phone wrapped in a small hand towel. She picks it up at the third round of the melody, and answers. "Hello?"

"Have you done as I have asked, sister Holly?"

"I have, Reverend Cranston."

"Bless you, child, you've done well."

"As you commanded."

"I command nothing, sister Holly. Only the Lord commands."

"Yes, Reverend Cranston," replies Holly softly. "I will do as He asks of me."

"God bless you. You destroyed the painting?"

"I spray-painted it. It's totally damaged and worthless."

The Reverend pauses. "You did not rip it apart?"

"No, but it's ruined. No one will want that thing hanging in their living room," replies Holly.

"This art crowd...this satanic, communist trash may have the means to repair the painting. I've seen them restore old paintings and make them look as good as when they were first made!"

"I'm sorry, Reverend Cranston. What should I do?"

"Don't do anything yet. Maybe this sinner will see the light and repent by destroying the remains of his worthless pile of so-called, art!"

Before Holly can respond, Reverend Cranston hangs up. She stares at her phone and shrugs her shoulders in confusion. Suddenly, Holly lets out a gasp when the television station cuts to a female reporter standing in front of the art gallery...her art gallery. She slides across the bed to the fairly nice television set for a cheap rental and looks around for the channel changer.

"Where's the remote!"

Unable to find the one, Holly manually turns up the volume and listens attentively as the reporter speaks excitedly into her hand-held microphone.

"Last night someone broke into the city's newest and most

trendy art gallery. A controversial painting titled Jesus, the Teenage Years, was nearly destroyed by vandals who left behind a very provocative statement spray-painted on the painting."

The reporter walks past the yellow crime scene tape at the entrance and into the gallery and continues her dialogue while climbing the stairs. Upon reaching the landing, she dramatically turns her head to a small group of cops and the bearded beatnik guy she remembers as the gallery owner. All of them inspect the damaged painting with the words, "Heresy" spray-painted in bright red paint on a large canvas area.

Holly scoots closer to the screen and sees the artist standing off to the side with his arms crossed, looking deep in thought.

The camera turns to the artist as the reporter shoves the microphone to his mouth. "May I ask why someone would want to destroy your art?"

"Because you're an idiot!" shouts Holly.

"Well, it's certainly a surprising response to the painting," says the artist calmly. "I've obviously touched a nerve here, but I don't think the vandalism destroyed the painting. In fact, I kind of like it even better. The painting was my statement, and the response is…well, it's interesting."

The reporter chuckles, "So, you think it's okay to deface art if you don't like it?"

"No, it's not right to destroy anyone's property. If this was a Biblical response to the art, I'm sure they're guilty of breaking some kind of commandment. But I do find myself liking the message. As much as I was pleased with the painting, I had a nagging feeling that something was missing. Most artists are overly critical of their work, as am I, but this negative gesture depicts a narrative that was lacking in the original; the violent death of Jesus for crimes against the establishment, and the suffering and wars perpetrated in his name throughout history. I hadn't captured that institutional violence. You might not agree with me on this, but I think it's an improvement."

Holly stares at the television utterly dumbfounded. Also, the time on the screen tells her that it's five o'clock and she's watching the afternoon news program. More disturbing is that her act of vandalism did not achieve the result she had hoped for. Worse is the artist's smarmy attitude that makes her blood boil.

What kind of a half-baked idiot is this guy? she thinks. When the reverend finds out, holy shit will hit the fan, which makes Holly laugh to herself. She should be more respectful she knows, but she also deserves a little lightheartedness in her life, too; especially after all she has been through in the past day. Reverend Cranston has a small and loyal army of the faithful glued to their computers surfing the Internet searching for crimes against God. He will find out about this, that is for certain, and he will not be happy.

The artist's face nearly covers the screen when the camera zooms in and he looks directly into the lens and says. "Why have most of us never thought about Jesus as a teenager? All I've done is create a painting, a modern interpretation of the missing years of Jesus, which oddly parallels our own lives. I used a modern term to describe this period of his life that has infuriated some intolerant, uptight wackos. What, you can't call Jesus a teenager? It's not what I was expecting; it's better than expected."

"Oh, you evil shithead!" screams Holly and buries her head in her hands, and worries how Reverend Cranston will react. He will find some method, as he has done on other occasions, to silence any critics of the Bible. As a soldier in God's army, she will do what is asked of her, but that doesn't mean she wants to. She takes a deep breath and huffs in frustration as she looks around the drab little room she calls home. The crusader for Christ, the loyal Watchman throws her cell phone on the bed, stomps across the room, and yells, "I've got to get out of this dump!"

She throws open the door and is greeted by the late afternoon sun nearly blinding her when it hits her right in the eyes.

"Arrgh!" she yells and slams the door shut.

Holly finds the cloud-free, late afternoon skies and balmy weather a pleasant change of scenery as she makes her way to the beach. She's smiling like a blissed-out hippy as she remembers dreaming about a winter's day like this whenever her mom played the Mamas and Papas, *California Dreaming* on her old record player. She wishes her mom were still alive and could see her now—the middle of December and it's sunny enough for Holly to take off her shoes and socks and walk across the warm sand to the edge of the Pacific Ocean.

Seagulls dive bomb just offshore for fish, while sandpipers, seemingly oblivious to her, busy themselves poking at the wet sand for food. Fifty yards from the water's edge, a group of young adults is gathered around a bonfire at the base of a small cliff. Holly can almost make out a story one of them is telling about a horrible teacher at school. She could walk over and join them if she wanted. Heck, she's not much older than they are, and she looks young for her age. But she's experienced too much in the past few years to be comfortable giggling with them about school and teachers.

"Race you to the water!" yells one of the girls.

Holly watches with a little pang of envy as two of the girls jump up and sprint across the beach to the ocean. Before they hit the shoreline they throw their towels onto the sand, pull off their sweatshirts and pants, and dive headfirst into a small wave after galloping through shallow water. Both are beautiful California trim and fit; nothing like the girls she grew up with back home in Indiana. Being athletic she's in good shape and was never as soft and fleshy as some of her friends, but these girls have beach volleyball bodies.

The girls pop up from the foamy whitewater, screaming in shock. "Holy shit! It's freezing!"

"My head is going to explode! Let's get out of here!"

They run out of the water laughing and pushing each other while racing to be the first one back to the towels. Holly watches as they dry off and hurriedly wrap their large towels around their torsos before ungracefully plopping down onto the sand. They're too far away for her to hear the details of their chattering, but she can make out something about "feeling sorry for people in Ohio."

"Let's get back to the fire!" suggests one of the girls as she quickly jumps to her feet and sprints back to the bonfire. Her friend takes her time drying her hair before pulling on her sweats and shaking the sand off her damp towel. She takes a moment of quiet meditation to look at the late afternoon sun on the horizon, then slowly starts walking across the sand lost in thought.

Encouraged by the girl's daring, Holly rolls up her pant legs and cautiously makes her way into the water. Immediately, a stabbing, prickly pain shoots from her toes to her shins, and she lets out a yelp. She's stunned and wonders how the two girls even dared to dive in headfirst—this water is icy cold!

Up on the beach, Holly hears a girl scream, "Stop it, Evan!" She turns to the sound and sees a young man wrestling with the girl she was just watching.

"You know you want it, Mimi," says the boy.

The girl struggles with her attacker, hitting him on the back and face with her fists while he clumsily paws at her breasts and smothers her in sloppy kisses that she turns her head away to avoid them. "You asshole! Fucking get off me!" she shouts.

The attack catches Holly completely off guard. First, there's the shock followed by fear—survival instincts that can overtake one without warning. It also means she's slow to run and rescue the girl in distress. She tries to yell out, but can only gasp instead.

Amid her confused response, she looks down at her feet, and as inappropriate as it is at this moment, she thinks, "Wow, the water's not freezing anymore. "

To the artist–

Blasphemy is another story. There are some things
that are not too clear, but that picture is lustful and
a disgrace to the faith. Consider this and what you
do from here is your business.

–anonymous letter writer

TIM'S QUIET DAY
AT THE BEACH

I was eagerly looking forward to a quiet evening at the beach watching the sunset after my tour of duty in Iraq. I was told a few things about the war before I enlisted, but I hadn't a clue about how loud and violent it truly was going to be. You can't imagine how terrifying it is—the screaming of low-flying jets before they dump their payloads, then the impact of tremendous explosions tearing into buildings and bodies. What follows next is an eerie silence you have to cover up as rocks, air conditioners, bicycles, and whatever else had been sent skyward rain down out of the smoke and dust and crashes to the ground.

Before joining the Marines I had heard all the stories from Desert Storm and Vietnam War vets, about how war changes you, mostly for the worst. But I felt I owed something to those New York City victims, who could only sit at their desks helplessly watching the planes speeding toward them, and the courageous firemen and policemen who raced into the towers to rescue any survivors. If there was a warning at the entrance that read, "You will die if you enter," I think they would have gone in anyway in the hopes of saving at least one person.

I don't think the war permanently damaged me, and most of my friends tell me that I haven't changed all that much. It's just that once in a while, I'd like a little peace.

A group of college students partying near the bluff was

disturbing the solitude I was seeking, but it looked like they were having fun. Before the war, I would have been there with them warming myself around a blazing campfire, surrounded by friends after a day of surfing. But now? I don't think they'd be comfortable with me, the freshly returned war vet. People have a difficult time handling certain subjects—cancer, death, and war veterans. God forbid someone should ask me what the war was like and I start talking about it—they might even find me a little scary.

I laugh at myself, Jesus, I guess I am a little damaged.

What I missed most while I was in Iraq was the ocean. I didn't even think about it when I enlisted, but the more I was away from it, the more I found myself dreaming about it. I spent my entire youth surfing and only lost my stoke when the water got too crowded. I remember how much fun it used to be, and as I got older, I realized I never fully appreciated the transcendental qualities of being in the ocean and riding waves. The surfer is free from life on land and the pressures of modern life—there's nothing like hours spent blissing out in a blue ocean. Iraq on the other hand was just brown. Two or three times a week, dust storms would hit like a hurricane and turn everything even browner.

Yesterday I placed an order for a mini-longboard, and as soon as I get it, I'm back in the water. Blue will become my favorite color again and I'll just have to deal with being a kook. Hopefully, I won't get harassed by some local hotshots because I've ruined a wave he could've shredded on.

"Evan, get off me!"

There's a certain tone of a voice in danger—more breath to it with a bit of gasping. I'm up and running toward the sound of a female yelling for help before I'm aware of doing so, racing quickly toward a guy attacking an unwilling girl a short distance away. He doesn't see me coming because he has his hands full as the girl is pounding him in the face with her free elbow, and doing a pretty good job of fighting him off.

I yank the guy off her and throw him hard to the sand. He's startled and confused, and I see his nose is bleeding and he has a large red welt over his eye. For a second I think, did I already hit him? In my moment of hesitation, the guy jumps to his feet and charges me. He's not a fighter and he's also pretty drunk, so I easily sidestep him and slam him to the ground again.

"Motherfucker!" he screams and attempts another futile charge. For a moment I'm almost laughing at him while dodging this idiot like a Spanish bullfighter. After a few charges, I step to the side and throw him down face-first into the sand pin his arms behind his back, and sit on him.

He tries to twist out from under me, but I've got all my weight on him and I'm pulling his arms behind his back toward me. I could snap his back or easily dislocate his shoulder if I wanted. But I'm not a killer, I was only trained to be one.

While I'm doing my best to calm the guy, the girl has to leap up and run to block three or other boys sprinting across the beach to rescue their friend yelling, "You're fucking dead, asshole!"

I'm outnumbered, but none of them look like they really want to fight. The girl easily holds them back by blocking them with her arms. "Leave him alone you guys," she pleads. "He's helping me!"

It all ends quickly when I get off the guy's back. He's pissed, but more than that, he's embarrassed and ashamed.

The girl is pretty calm for just being attacked. "Jesus, Evan. What are you thinking?"

"I'm so sorry, Mimi," he mumbles.

One of the girls yells at Evan. "Evan, you're a piece of shit!"

The girl, who I now know as Mimi, calmly takes control and tells Evan, "Please go home. You've been drinking too much and you're totally out of control! Just go home. Please!"

Mimi and I watch Evan slowly make his way across the beach with the guys and girls. I can hear them scolding him the entire way to the campfire. The girls stand guard with their arms crossed while Evan and another boy pack up his belongings and leave.

"Make sure he gets home in one piece!" Mimi calls out to the boy helping Evan. He acknowledges her request with a nod and a wave.

Mimi takes hold of my arm and says, "I'm so sorry you had to get involved. Are you okay? Did he hit you?"

"Not a scratch. Who was that jerk anyway?"

"I'm embarrassed to admit it, but he's my old boyfriend. He's a good guy," she tells me, "but he's been partying and drinking a lot recently. But hey, thanks for coming to my rescue. What's your name?"

God, she's really cute, I think as I stand like a mute staring at her and taking way too long to give her my name.

"Your name? You're going to tell me, aren't you?"

I finally manage to stumble out, "Tim. Tim Valdez."

She holds out her hand. "I'm Mimi."

"I sort of figured that one out," I laugh.

Now she's the one staring at me...waiting...puzzled that I'm not engaged in any further conversation. She looks down at our hands, I'm still holding hers, but I can feel her pulling away slightly.

"Well...thanks again," she says.

I let go of her hand and watched her walk back to her friends. I return to my spot on the beach and look over my shoulder to see if Mimi is doing the same. She isn't. They've headed back to their bonfire, and Tim Valdez is history. His heroics will just be a story they'll laugh about around another campfire on the beach.

I'm such a dipshit, I think. Flopping onto my towel I wrap my arms around my knees and close my eyes to clear my head. I can usually block out the world in a second but the adrenaline from the fight has kicked into action, so now I've also got a new brain worm rolling around in my head, dipshit, dipshit.

Eventually, I got back to thinking about my new board and recalled a great surf trip to Mexico with a few friends, which was my last surf session before boot camp. I remember being extremely fatalistic about the kind of horror I would be facing in Iraq, and I ended up surfing like it was going to be the last time I would ever ride a wave. Even my friends remarked on how fearless my surfing was. I recall that after five days of maniacal surfing, and throwing caution to the wind on every ride, I didn't blow one wave. I don't think I even fell off once.

"Hey ... Tim.'"

Snapping out of my inner conversation, I open my eyes and find Mimi standing in front of me, silhouetted by the sun.

"Do you mind if I join you?"

"Oh, yeah, sure. Please"

Mimi lays her towel out on the sand and I can't help but notice how gracefully she folds her legs to sit down cross-legged.

"Thanks again for the heroics.," she smiles.

Once again I'm at a loss for words. I notice a small sandbar a hundred yards away up the beach and ask her. "Would you like to walk with me up that little peak? I see some kids are suiting up and getting ready to surf it."

Mimi, and looks up the beach to the spot I'm pointing at.

"Sure. It looks like your social skills are returning."

She offers her hand and I help her stand up, and I like the feel of her hand which is cool. I also can't help but notice her well-shaped legs when I bend down to pick up her towel and knock the sand off.

Along the way, Mimi picks up a broken sand dollar shell and tosses it into a wave. She's talking about her old boyfriend Evan and how they grew apart when she was away—him staying at home, hanging out with his friends, not growing up, and drinking too much.

I think to myself, *maybe we need to bring back the draft and give young people something to do while we're waiting for them to grow up. They could be helping out the poor and homeless, and doing something productive with their lives.*

Evan sounds like a self-absorbed whiner. He doesn't interest me at all, except that Mimi was involved with him at one point in her life, so maybe he might have some redeeming qualities.

Mimi senses that her conversation about Evan is going on too long and says, "I'm sorry. I'm boring you with my stupid ex-boyfriend stuff, aren't I?" she asks.

"Where did you learn to fight like that?" I ask.

Mimi laughs, "I went to an all-girls Catholic high school."

"Really?" I ask.

Mimi laughs and replies, "Really? This looks like a good spot, at least the sand is dry."

We sit quietly for a moment, and stare at a well-shaped little peak. I think about its life that began five thousand miles away, crossing the ocean with other fellow waves, and in its final moment as it nears the shore, it crests and ends this life as a small thumping shore pound. I wish I knew what Mimi was thinking. We're two strangers sitting on the beach staring at the horizon and waiting for the sun to set. We know nothing about each other, except I think she's really cute and I know her old boyfriend tried to rape her and I kicked his ass. This is certainly a good foundation to base a friendship on, I joke to myself with a chuckle.

"What's so funny?" asks Mimi.

I lie. "An all-girls Catholic school? That's hilarious."

"If you only knew our nuns, and I'm not kidding!"

That's a good conversation starter, Tim. Anything else?

She's smiling at me, waiting...

"I guess I'm not used to this," I finally say.

"Sitting next to a girl?" laughs Mimi.

"No. Well, actually, yes. I've only been home for a few weeks and this is just so different from where I was."

"Home from where?"

"Iraq."

"You were in Iraq? I'm sorry, I mean, that must have been pretty rough, right?"

"Don't worry. I wasn't such a basket case before I left."

"I think you're doing great. Plus, you saved me. That counts for a lot, don't you think? No need to apologize."

"Thanks for being so understanding. My last tour was pretty rough, and as much as I don't like to admit it, I think it affected me more than I care to believe."

"You don't have to talk about it if you don't want to."

I hesitate and instead of putting Mimi at ease, I'm doing just the opposite. Who wants to hear shit about the war from a guy you've just met? And, let's face it, she just witnessed me being kind of violent even though it was to save her.

I try to think about another subject we could talk about, but what? We turn away from each other and watch two teenage boys charge across the beach with incredibly short surfboards under their arms and run into the small surf without any hesitation.

"We could change the topic if you want," says Mimi. "Or, you can talk about it. I'm a very good listener."

"Most people don't want to hear about this. Have you ever been in a war zone?"

"Only for a couple of days," answers Mimi.

Is she kidding me again? "You were? Where was that?"

"I'll tell you all about it once you tell me a little bit about Iraq, Okay? What have you got to lose, Tim?"

"Okay then, let's start at the low point...and a little girl. She was maybe four years old at most."

Mimi leans away from me a bit and says, "Oh dear, this might be more than I asked for. But please continue, I'm cool."

"Stop me when you've heard more than you care to. It's not like I did anything horrible, it was an event that unfortunately happened all too regularly over there."

Mimi takes my hand and gives it a gentle squeeze. "Okay Tim, I'm here for the duration. So, tell me about this, *event.*"

I stumble, searching for a way to start, but I'm finding it difficult. I'm not a storyteller, to begin with, so how does one start a story properly?

Mimi senses my inability to get the words out. "Just go for it," she smiles. "Once you get rolling it gets a lot easier. Trust me, I had presented a term paper to a crowd of professors whose sole purpose was to find flaws in my research and fail me."

I take a deep breath and begin. "It was on my last tour. War in general can be boring. You sit around doing nothing for days until suddenly, the shit hits the fan. On this day we watched our jets unload tons of bombs onto the city. Everyone cheered and laughed as huge fireballs lit up the sky, but none of us had a clue as to what we had just done.

I stop and hesitate. I don't cry anymore, at least not like I used to whenever I thought about it.

"Tim, are you okay?"

"What? Oh yeah, sure. At any rate, a couple of hours after the bombing ended, we began patrolling the area, and when we saw the damage we had done, everyone went numb. We just blew them up—everything, until there was hardly anything left standing. We turned an entire city to dust. Saddam should have known what kind of madmen he was dealing with."

"Oh my god," sighs Mimi.

Whenever I tell this story, I can't help but put myself in the Iraqi's position—to see their homes, the ancient city disintegrating into dust from powerful explosives dropped from aircraft that are killing or injuring friends, family, and neighbors. One minute they're walking home from the market or work, and then suddenly buildings are blowing apart all around them.

"We weren't surprised at the destruction. We knew this was going to happen because it was our Captain who called in the coordinates and we were very close to the city. After the bombing, we began searching for survivors, but mostly for insurgents hiding among the ruins waiting to ambush us. When you're on patrol, every second might be your last, so you're on high alert for any movement or sound. My attention to detail and the sound was profound despite gunships flying overhead and other firefights elsewhere in the city."

I turn away from Mimi because if I don't take a breath, I'll start crying—and I don't want to in front of this sweet girl."

Mimi is silent, sitting with her eyes cast downward staring at the sand running through her fingers.

"Are okay so far?" I ask.

She looks up and offers me an understanding smile. "So far, so good."

After a deep breath, I continue. "As I came near to what was once an apartment building, I picked up a quiet whimper coming from a pile of rubble and quickly moved in even though my guys were yelling at me to take it slow.

I got to the voice, shouldered my weapon, and began removing a pile of concrete blocks. After some digging, I spotted a bloodied arm sticking out of the rubble. It was a child's hand scraping at the broken concrete, trying to move it aside. I laid down my weapon and pack and removed enough debris to gently pull her out. But she was resisting me, crying and trying to pull away from my grip. I figured she was in shock and it took me several moments before I realized she had a tight grip with her other hand on a hand buried deeper in the rubble. I finally freed her and tended to her wounds before taking her to the hospital, one of the few buildings we hadn't destroyed. I carried her past a long line of injured civilians and I wondered why we had to destroy so much just to get one guy out of power. Most of these people were not bothering anyone until we arrived. Then they found themselves running for their lives as the world around them began disintegrating."

CALIFORNIA DREAMIN'

The attack on the young woman ended quickly when a young man rushed to her aid out of nowhere and yanked the attacker off the girl. Then, he tossed the guy to the ground a few times. She watched the entire event unfold and was annoyed at herself for hesitating to help. Fortunately, it ended well, and now the small waves are lapping at her legs and the salty ocean is rejuvenating her weary spirit. After a few minutes in the ocean, she marvels at how much warmer it is the longer you're in it. Returning to her towel she dries her feet and legs and brushes the sand out from between her toes. Then she rubs her hands over her feet and heels and is surprised at how smooth they are—nature's pedicure.

"Sand is so much better than mud," she tells herself. It's not long though before her feet begin tingling as she begins to thaw out and the blood flow returns. The water had not warmed up at all; she had only been numb to its deathly grip.

Holly looks over to the young stranger sitting alone on the beach staring out at the ocean. I should go over and talk to him, she thinks. He's pretty cute and maybe he's a Christian too. I could at least tell him what a heroic act he did, getting that guy off that poor girl.

Holly knows her little vacation is just a diversion from the task at hand. She needs to call Reverend Cranston and tell him her destruction of the painting hasn't turned out as planned.

"All because of that stupid artist," she complains out loud.

It was a troubled conversation Holly had with herself on her walk from the beach to her little dark apartment. The moment she opened the door, she huffed out an exasperated breath when she picked up her cell phone and discovered she had seven messages. And who else would be calling except the Reverend who must have heard the news.

Holly picks up her phone, locates the reverend in her contacts, and then taps his icon.

"Greetings, Sister Holly. I see your efforts last night were not as effective as you might have hoped for."

"That artist is as dense as a stone and didn't take the hint. He should be easy to find though."

"I had hoped it would not have come to this. Do you have your weapon with you?"

"I do," says Holly. "It's under my bed."

"That painting is a foul and evil creation. The Lord does not allow agents of Satan to mock Him. The sword is the only course of action available. God bless you, Holly. Call me when this task is complete."

Holly pulls up the bed skirt, removes a custom canvas bag, and lays it on the bed. She unzips the bag and carefully pulls out her crossbow—not an ordinary crossbow, like one that anyone buys at Walmart for ninety-nine bucks. Hers is a carbon laminated, Barnett Ghost 410 that Reverend Cranston bought for her upon learning she was the Indiana state high-school archery champion. Holly holds the bow to her cheek and smells its unique odor, and she isn't ashamed to admit that she loves her crossbow. She not only appreciates the sleek engineering and deadly accuracy but to use it effectively, she had to stop drinking. After her mother died and Holly descended into despair, it was her crossbow that brought her back to life—a sober life in the light of the Lord.

Holly has used her crossbow on squirrels and small game. *Thou shalt not kill is the most important commandment,* thought Holly, until Reverend Cranston instructed her that there are other commandments even more important to God, such as; Thou shalt have no other gods before me. One of his favorites he loves to say is: Thou shalt not make unto thee any graven image or any likeness of anything that is in heaven above, or that is in the earth beneath, or that is in the water under the earth. Thou shalt not bow down thyself to them, nor serve them: for I the Lord thy God am a jealous God, visiting the iniquity of the fathers upon the children unto the third and fourth generation of them that hate me.

Reverend Cranston taught her those words, and as much as she appreciates his knowledge of the Bible, she always thought that God sent Jesus to Earth to show us how much God loved us.

While she fine-tunes her weapon, Holly turns to the Teenage Jesus print and frowns. The artist who created this image has sealed his pact with Satan. How could he have thought for one second that Jesus Christ would be hanging out with the town whore wearing gold coins for a headband with her breast exposed? If he had only opened and read the Bible, he might have read that there are many warnings about nakedness and showing off.

Because of the artist's blasé attitude, she saw on television, it's apparent he intentionally produced a sinful image that has offended God and His followers. For these transgressions, he must pay the price.

This painting is blasphemy! Jesus would of never been in a position such as you depicted in your painting. It says he was tempted, yet without sin. Your painting shows sin and even playing with sin, not temptation. Any sort of looking upon nakedness was and still is sin. Sure, give in... instead of grieving and weeping over our culture. I think the seducing spirits promised during the end times have seduced you. You might ought to fall on your face before a holy God and be sure you haven't changed the meaning of scripture...there is a huge consequence for that!

Grieved and broken over this,

-Gail Johnson

MARY OF MAGDALA

Her land near the Sea of Galilee had not known a moment's peace for many years. Public officials made fortunes from outlaws and bandits who roamed the countryside and when apprehended, were quickly released from jail once a "consideration" was made. It is said that nobody remained in prison very long except the poor. Ongoing bloody battles between warring Jewish sects affect even the most remote villages, and when they aren't fighting amongst themselves, they're attacking Gentile settlements and Roman garrisons. Major roads are filled with crosses hung with the executed, announcing to any who choose to fight the power of Rome, that crucifixion will be their last act of protest. Assassinations are common. Sicaru, zealots who specialize in the knife, mingle among the marketplace crowds with their intended victim, usually one considered a disloyal Jew, stab them with a deep thrust in the back then quickly disappear.

The recently orphaned, eighteen-year-old Mary finds herself nearly alone on her deceased father's vast country estate after he died unexpectedly the previous year. Many consider a young woman incapable of managing an estate of this size, but in truth, they all have their eyes on the property and her sizable dowry.

Under the canopy of an open terrace at her hilltop villa, Mary gazes at a dark sky filled with a billion stars on this moonless night, lounging on a comfortable couch surrounded by embroidered cushions and soft pillows. Below the villa are groves of almond, orange, and olive trees that brought great wealth to her father. But tonight her attention is fixed on the calm waters of the Sea of Galilee far below, mirroring the sky above. Since childhood, it amused her to compare the lights of the small villages and large estates built by man, pitiful when compared to the lights of heaven. A single candle fighting the dark in this mountainous landscape seems like a lopsided battle against the vast, infinite universe.

Mary's handmaiden, a young woman named Sarah, kneels nearby folding clothing, while carefully packing an ornately carved wooden chest. She stops her work and asks Mary, "What are you thinking?"

Mary sighs, "I was wondering if I shall ever feel happiness again, and if will I ever see more of the world than my little village."

Mary rises and walks to a large pile of clothing covering her bed and begins folding a dress before gently laying it into the chest. She kneels next to her handmaiden and says, "Sarah, we will have many great adventures, wait and see. Imagine being free from the prying eyes of the priests and those spoiled, bothersome rich men's sons. We know all too well what their sole desire is."

"To lay their hands on your father's treasure," says Sarah.

"If they bed me, shouldn't that be an even greater treasure?" laughs Mary.

"Such is our life, Mary. The custom of marriage is as old as the earth itself. At least you might have a chance of marrying into a good family. My choices are non-existent."

"Nonsense, Sarah! Unlike me, you will find a handsome man and marry for love. Maybe he will have a good trade or a farm with orchards and livestock."

"A shepherd's wife? Living in poverty with filthy animals? I would rather stay with you and remain unmarried."

"Stay with me, then," says Mary. "Maybe there is a young man for you in Joppa."

"I do not look forward to that city," replies Sarah. "They say the Romans rule there with a cruelty unknown to us."

"They couldn't be any more dangerous than the thieves that roam the countryside. Imagine the sea at our doorstep. A body of water that stretches beyond our imaginations. Doesn't that sound wonderful?"

"Yes, I suppose it does. I have never seen the great sea."

"There are no limits to what two young women can do. I look forward to our new life."

The sun is slow to rise over the sea before old Joppa. After a long journey with many nights spent in roadside inns, the new visitors are shocked before entering through the city gates as they pass through some of the most miserable and poor neighborhoods they have ever witnessed.

"My goodness, Mary, I have never seen such poverty before," says Sarah, covering her nose with her scarf. "How can this happen when so much wealth is in abundance?"

"We should not allow this if we are true citizens of the world, Sarah. Once we settle in, you and I will make every effort to share our good fortune with those in need."

"Is this to be our new adventure?"

"Yes. We shall not be two selfish girls waiting for a husband to lord over our lives after stealing our dowry. Instead, our task will be to help those in need by feeding and caring for them."

Once they clear a brief inspection of their cart which is

loaded with wooden boxes filled with Mary and Sarah's clothing, household goods, and a few small pieces of furniture, the Roman soldiers allow Mary's cart to pass through the gates of the ancient port city. They move slowly through the city's nearly empty streets sitting beside the driver with their heads and shoulders covered, although some of Mary's long red hair manages to escape and flow down her back.

Curious merchants setting up their stalls briefly stop their tasks for a look at the passersby. They make snap judgments about the strangers before turning back to their work, maybe wondering who the beautiful red-haired young woman might be. Two guards walking alongside the cart stay busy brushing away a few filthy waifs, who laugh and run alongside them, begging the riders to throw down a few coins.

The cart turns onto a wide boulevard, and the sight before them takes Mary and Sarah's breath away. A large synagogue is casting a long, dark shadow over the length of the street, and patiently waiting in the dark are dozens of goats, bleating lambs, calves, and their vendors who will sell them for pennies a pound to the synagogue's money changers. Pigeons in cages gently coo and also wait their turn to be sold for the sacrifice—offerings to be slaughtered as protection from a vengeful God.

As Mary's cart draws nearer to the synagogue the stench fills the atmosphere with a dreadful odor. Sarah gags in response and covers her nose with her tunic as a small army of men with buckets of water, mops, and shovels fill boxes with blood and intestinal slime from the previous day's offerings before loading the boxes onto dozens of carts that will carry the refuse far away from this place of worship.

The noisy children running alongside the cart desert them as they enter the city and the darkened boulevard is fortunately left behind when the cart bursts into the sunshine and fresh air. Within a few blocks, the girls enter a neighborhood of elegant homes hidden behind large stone walls that are covered with bougainvillea, grape vines, and flowers. They slow before passing through the iron gates of a large estate as a group of workers scatter off to the side of the drive and gawk at the young women with bewildered interest. The cart makes its way up a long drive past well-manicured hedges, flowering gardens, and ponds. Finally, they reach the entry of the main house which has a commanding view of the city below.

Their host, Joseph of Arimathea, a business partner of Mary's deceased father, is waiting for them on the portico with open arms and a wide smile. But even at the entrance, there is scaffolding, piles of bricks, and an army of workers walking in and out of the house with tools and buckets of mortar. Those working inside the house make a deafening racket with their chisels, saws, and hammers.

After such an arduous journey through hostile lands, barren desert, and the synagogue's horrible stench, Sarah is disappointed by the condition of their her home.

Hoping to cheer her friend, Mary turns to her and whispers, "Do not forget those outside the gates, Sarah. We will be living in luxury in comparison, but I do hope there is some livable space for us somewhere in this chaos."

Sorry to hear this! Christians can be the most horrible
people at times but also can be the most kind.
Remember that Jesus often came up against
hostility during his ministry, so please don't be
disheartened and keep your art going. I'm sure God
has his hand on it! I've told a few people about your
painting, and they all had positive comments to make.
Yours in Christ

-Anderson

JESUS, THE TEENAGE YEARS

In a partially remodeled bathing room, Judas and I are struggling as we attempt to install a Roman-styled sink. The glazed ceramic basin is nearly in place, but we are having a difficult time lining it up with the lead drain pipe designed to take water from the basin through the pipe and out to a sewage pond. At the moment, we're under the wood framing holding up the sink, covered in grime and cursing the Roman architect who created this monster. Yesterday he presented us with what he said were simple installation instructions. If he were here today, Judas has promised to strangle him with those same simple instructions.

Judas curses, "Satan has created this monstrosity to drive workers mad. Damn this thing!"

"What is wrong with wells and buckets? We have plenty of poor and unemployed to fetch water," I reply.

"Because workers cost money. They eat and drink...and they demand decent housing!"

"Interesting, brother, maybe this plumbing the Romans are so fond of is a plan to drive us deeper into despair by taking away our livelihoods."

I lift the end of the frame a bit higher to level the sink, while Judas braces the heavy marble with his shoulder.

"Damn this infernal device!" shouts Judas.

From the corner of my eye, I see we are being spied upon.

Uncle Joseph's children, a seven-year-old boy, and his younger sister are listening to us just outside the door. I see them poking each other and giggling, then gasp in shock when Judas yells, "Shit! I'm going to kill the inventor of this piece of crap!"

I laugh out loud when I see them turn and run through the house with their high-pitched voices echoing, "Father! Father!"

We continue our struggle with a few more attempts to secure the sink in place. The sink is finally in place and I look down at my hands to see they are scratched and bloody.

I hear a woman's laugh behind us and watch Judas scramble out from under the sink, nearly knocking me over in the process. We stand and brush off the dirt and find a well-dressed, young woman with dark red hair and large green eyes standing before us with a wide smile and her hands on her hips shaking her head disapprovingly. At her side are my two young cousins, James and Anna, wagging their fingers and giggling.

The young woman mocks us. "You two must be jesters from a traveling circus. I have never heard such a commotion in my life!"

She grabs two cloth towels lying nearby and places them in a bucket of water lying nearby. "Shame on you! There are children here!" she scolds while handing us the towels.

I am mortified and embarrassed as I wipe my face and drop my head in shame. "Forgive us, please. We did not realize anyone was nearby."

It is impossible not to notice that the beautiful red-haired girl is staring at me and her cheeks flushed. *But in this heat,* I think, *whose cheeks are not flushed*?

The young woman lowers her eyes and calms her tone. "It is difficult enough getting them to pay attention to their lessons without you two cursing every God under the sun."

She takes hold of my niece and nephew's hands, and quietly says, "Please, less commotion. Come, children." Then, just as quickly as she appeared, she pivots and leaves. I take notice that she briefly paused at the doorway and turned slightly in my direction. It's even possible I saw her eyes brighten as she gave me a warm smile.

Judas grins. "She smiled at you, did you see?"

I smile while nodding in agreement. "Did you notice her eyes and how they glowed like emeralds? I hope that is not the last time she reprimands us." I roll the damp towel in my hands and wipe my face.

"Eyes like emeralds?" laughs Judas. "You are already in love!"

"Of course, I am," I joke. "But who is she, and why is she here, and in my uncle's home? Maybe she is bound to a wealthy but cruel prince, and desires to be rescued."

"You should come to her aid, then," encourages Judas.

"I will sacrifice all I have to free her from her masters."

"It is a courageous undertaking, brother. And even though her father and an army of suitors may pursue you, they will never find your place of hiding."

I laugh and reply, "The hills above Galilee will be our haven. There we will grow old and fat together."

"With such a beauty lying beneath you, I see many sons and daughters!"

"Many! And she will roast the finest meats and bake the softest breads" I exclaim.

"If you feed me, I will watch the children while you and your fat little beauty sneak off to make love in a secret cave."

The following day, Mary returns to the bathing area where the handsome young man was cursing and carrying on with his rough-looking companion, but the bath is empty of workers. The beautiful marble sink the two were struggling with has been installed—embedded into the stone countertop featuring elaborate lead fixtures. She feels disappointed, and even displeased by his disappearance, and credits the heat made more unbearable by the lack of wind that has her agitated.

A light tapping sound draws her attention to a nearby room and Mary carefully makes her way through the dust-covered hallway past a few freshly plastered rooms and then peers through a partially opened heavy wooden door. Her eyes focus on a strong, sweat-covered hand holding a small iron nail against a wooden cabinet. The hand violently slams the hammer onto the nail head once and drives it deep into the wood, and the power and force of the movement cause her to flinch and gasp out loud. The young man looks up at her and lays his hammer down to turn his back to wipe the sweat and dirt off his face. Mary takes notice, not only of his muscular arms and his lean, strong torso, but she also thinks, *he is so uninhibited with his nakedness.* It makes her laugh quietly to herself.

I hear quiet laughter and turn away from my work to find the young woman from yesterday watching me. I lay down my hammer and wipe away the grime and sweat, aware that she might even be studying me. It almost makes me laugh because she was so full of herself yesterday. Today, it will be my turn to take the high road, so I turn to her quickly and face her with a wide smile.

She blushes red from embarrassment and stutters, "Am I... uh...interrupting your labor?"

"No, not at all," I reply. "And I must apologize for our cursing yesterday, but your Roman architect gave us no instructions."

"No apology is necessary. Despite my lecturing you, yesterday was the first time in many months I found myself able to laugh."

"I am glad to be of service, but why is that?"

"My father died and since that time I have been beset on all sides by greedy vultures who did not have the decency to allow me a few moments to grieve his death."

My playful moment evaporates when I recall my own father's death. "I am sorry for your loss. I know the pain of losing a father. The pain does not recede with time as many say. Are you Roman?"

"Thank you for your kind words, but no, I was born in Syria and raised in the region around Hippos, on the Sea of Galilee."

"But your clothing, it is Roman."

"I'm staying here because of the thieves, most of whom were my family. They forced me to abandon my home, and I was invited by Joseph to live here until my estate was settled."

"You are lucky then to have him as a friend. There is no one more caring and honest."

"Honest, yes, but he thinks my clothing is too modern, and I suspect he believes that as a woman, I am not capable of managing my affairs as a man might."

The young woman narrowed her eyes and pursed her lips. "I ran my father's business very well," she continues. "That is until I was harassed daily by the thieves. We shall see how well they do managing a vast estate with vineyards and livestock. Once they discover there is no gold or treasure, they will tire of the work and sell off bits and pieces until it is nothing more than a sad ruin."

"I did not mean to say you are not capable, only that men do not give women the respect we deserve, especially in business."

"It was all so unnecessary," says Mary. "I was willing to give everyone a fair share if they worked with me, but it was not good enough for them. There was much rancor and bickering, and these were family members. Thankfully, I was able to transfer most of the estate and titles into my accounts thanks to Joseph."

"You certainly seem capable of holding your own against anyone."

Mary softens and smiles, "The experience might have left me a little brittle. I am sorry if I seem brash." Mary bows her head slightly and says, "My name is Mary"

"I am called Jesus. We are remodeling my uncle's home as he felt it needed improvements. I am supervising the construction."

Mary is taken aback. "Joseph is your uncle?"

"Yes, he is my mother's uncle. Her name is also Mary."

"I have heard about your mother and her son from my father. Joseph has many good things to say about you."

"How have you come to be here?" I ask.

Mary replies, "Your Uncle Joseph was one of my father's business partners. They grew up together as children in the same household…and, I'm sorry, I mistook you for a slave."

"How were you to know? I am covered in filth and do slave's work."

While we talk I am continually wiping at the dust on my arms and face with the cloth to no avail. It is stuck to me like a paste

I point out the unfinished wood cabinet to Mary. "I am much better suited to working with wood. The complex Roman plumbing is too foreign to me."

Mary laughs, "But it is foreign!"

We laugh not because of the silly joke. I believe we are attracted to one another, and it creates some uncomfortable tension. Once the laughing subsides, I am at a loss for words and we face each other for a moment of silence.

Thankfully, Mary is a better conversationalist than I am. "I could use more lightheartedness in my life. My father was not a very humorous man. He was more interested in gathering land and amassing wealth."

"And you are not of a like mind?"

"I certainly hope not," she replies. "I am more interested in seeing our people fed. But since my father passed away, I have been besieged by many whose only goal is to remove the contents of my father's bank by wedding me."

"Greed brings out the worst in people. Still, it must be difficult to deal with the complex affairs of a large estate," I say.

"I would be lying if I said it is not difficult."

"I did not mean to imply that you are not up to the task as a young woman."

"As a female, I know how the men treat us; property to be bought and sold if some have their say. But my father taught me well, and I am as capable as any man. Many of these would-be suitors who have found their way into my life, I find disgusting. They desire a marriage contract solely to enrich their families. As if I would marry anyone who is a stranger to me."

"You will find many of the men in this city no different."

"It would please me if there were at least a few young men who feel as I do. I do not require a husband, as I have my work to keep me busy, and from what I have observed, I will have my hands full. I have never seen so much filth and poverty in my life until entering this city."

"Many of them were once landowners and farmers, but high taxes and the Roman's need for land have sent them into poverty. Many of the poor are honorable and hard-working—such as the men and boys I work with. Wait, what kind of work is it you do?"

"I help the poor and sick—those in need of clothing, food, and shelter. It is what I did in Hippos, but the slums in this city are far larger than I could have ever imagined."

The beautiful woman standing before me isn't the pampered spoiled girl I might have assumed had I seen her from a distance. She is caring and thoughtful, intelligent, and I am not blind, she is physically stunning. I doubt her many suitors were solely interested in her wealth.

"Why are you here as a worker?" asks Mary. "I understood the son of Joseph and Mary was quite a scholar, even in his youth. I thought you would have been studying to become a teacher or a senator."

I would tell Mary if I knew her better, how, after my Father died, I lost the desire to attend my lessons. Many of us having faced and survived disaster, have fallen into a darkness with no bottom, and my malady is no different. At present, I feel no desire to be the scholar many hoped I would become.

"Carrying on the tradition of carpentry is to honor the skills taught to me by my Father since childhood. The art of woodworking is a well-paid skill, and as wood is a rare and expensive commodity, journeymen carpenters are in great demand in this land."

I feel Mary might feel she has insulted me. When she comes to know me better she will understand that regardless of my scholarship, it is more important to me to keep my crew employed, fed, and clothed. I work hard, as do all my crew; but unlike many other builders who live in luxury while paying their workers' slave wages, I share equally with my workers.

"Plus," I add, "I enjoy working alongside my friends.."

Courtship is an elaborate and sometimes difficult social

game we play; teasing and play are followed by a long period of the chase. There can be many false starts before any serious affection between the lovers attaches itself to the heart. As our custom dictates, next is gift-bearing, and if one is worthy, acceptance and partnership. We are not even close to the first phase; we have only just been introduced.

"Forgive me," says Mary. "I am keeping you from your work."

I look at the cabinet and shrug. "There is always work, but I should return to it. I enjoyed meeting you."

"As did I," she replies before turning away and leaving.

There is a proper limit in society to unsupervised conversations between young people, especially when the young man is half-clothed. I am certain we exceeded that artificial period, but in that brief time, we discovered that we both care for those less fortunate than ourselves and have a healthy perspective on questioning tradition.

I listen to the sound of her sandals on the marble flooring as she moves away from my dusty workplace, and continue to listen until I cannot hear them any longer. I find myself unsettled that the moment has passed.

Take these eager lips and hold me fast...
I'm afraid this kind of joy can't last
How can we keep love alive
How can anything survive
When these little minds tear you in two...
...What a town without pity can do.

–Gene Pitney,
Town Without Pity

TIM AND MIMI

Two days have passed since the evening we first met. We walked on the beach and talked for hours almost non-stop, and I couldn't stop thinking about her. I learned that Mimi spent time in Central America helping poor Mayan women and almost got killed in an ambush by a right-wing corporate militia. Now she's working at a battered women's shelter, which had us both laughing because of me saving her from Evan who was trying to rape her. Now that I know her better, I wish I could have smacked him around a bit more to straighten his ass out.

We carried on until her friend Kristy came over and told us they were leaving and to wrap it up. I think we were surprised that we connected so well, and I know we both felt that something very interesting had taken place between us. When we got to her car, I leaned in to give her a quick kiss on the cheek, but instead, she gave me the sweetest kiss on the lips. I didn't know how to respond, so I clumsily asked her, "Should I take your phone number?"

"Yes Tim!" she laughed.

I spent the following days talking to her a lot in my mind, but I hesitated to make the call because some of those conversations were about how fucked up I was. And I don't want to screw this up.

I finally gathered up the nerve and calmed my breathing as I dialed her number and waited for her to answer.

"Hello?"

"Hi Mimi, it's Tim."

"Tim! I was hoping you were going to call. Why did you wait so long to call me?"

"I don't know. Just nerves, I guess."

"You too?" she laughs. "I've been thinking about you an awful lot. You are calling to see me again, right?"

"Yes. Definitely yes."

"What do you think?" she asks. "Dinner...show?"

"How about both?"

"When?"

"How about tonight?"

"Make it early," she says.

We went to a funky restaurant that had sawdust on the floor and was famous for its French dip sandwiches. It was Mimi's suggestion and although I was hoping for something more intimate, the food was great. Then we saw a well-reviewed movie that we felt might be good enough to get an Academy Award, but all I could think of was the moment we might share a second kiss. After the film, we stopped in front of her small apartment and I turned off the engine. I thought we might talk about the movie, but instead, we locked our lips together and stayed that way for a very long time before reluctantly parting ways.

Two days later we picked up steak burritos from a favorite taqueria and headed out to the beach to watch the sunset.

Mimi wipes a bit of guacamole off her lips and looks at me with a smile. "This sure is an improvement over last week."

It's two a.m. and I wake up to find Mimi staring at me in the dark. She has the sheet pulled up over her chest and is resting her head on her arm. The covers are lying on the floor and I'm freezing.

ppening on a
but I had to
on its own.
We spotted
at looked
at maybe
not, you
and I
out a

and after a few moments my
d I find one lying on the floor
of us and she scoots close and
raps her arm around my waist.
q once tonight," she says.
life, I'm letting go of that conversation

A

Tim, but I'm still curious why you were
tour was up. That's something you haven't

Do

n't want to hear it."

ould be the judge of that. You shouldn't hold stuff
good for you."

ght, I guess this is as good a time as any that she
out exactly who I am, good or bad. Where to start? My
ng about being duped by our government into thinking
s wanted us there to protect the world from Saddam and
ns of mass destruction?

Maybe I should begin with what my commander called me, "a
cken-shit deserter who was aiding the enemy." I called it, "daring
ravery and compassion under difficult conditions that resulted in the
lives of hundreds of people being saved from unnecessary slaughter.

I take a deep breath and begin my tale. "Imagine Mimi, that you are the enemy, the one who volunteered to travel to Guatemala to kill Mayans because of a lie told to you by your government. That's how I felt after a few months in Iraq. Every day after the air strikes, which continued almost non-stop, each time I wondered, just how many Iraqis did we kill this time? The smell of death was everywhere. It's over one hundred degrees all the time and there

are no services to handle the multitude of tragedies h[...]
grand scale because we destroyed it all. I hate to say i[...]
get used to it or go completely mad, which is pretty sic[...]

The end of the line came one day while on patrol. [...]
three guys running down a street carrying something t[...]
like an IED. We took off after them, carefully, thinking th[...]
it was a trap to lure us into an ambush. Then again, maybe[...]
just never know. But, I've got my weapon in firing positio[...]
have enough killing shit wrapped around my chest to wip[...]
small village."

"What's an IED?" she asks.

"It's an acronym for an Improvised Explosive Devic[...]
homemade mine or bomb."

I reach over and grab a nearby glass of water and ask, "[...]
you still want to hear this, Mimi?"

She takes the glass from me and sips the water slowly.

"Yeah, keep going."

"Okay, so we give chase and I caught up pretty quickly to
these guys—they weren't in fighting shape and I could tell they
were getting winded. I yelled to them, 'Stop motherfuckers or I will
shoot!' They quickly split up—two run down an alleyway, while
one of the guys freezes. I am truly ready to kill this guy for making
me run so damn far. That's how crazy the place made us—that I'd
kill them because I was pissed off at them for running away from
a madman who was chasing them with an automatic weapon and
hand grenades."

"Tim, that is so horrible," says Mimi.

"Yeah, it could have been. But stay with me, it has a happy
ending. The two other guys escaped, but my guy dropped to his
knees and began begging, 'surrender, surrender!' I yelled in Arabic,

'Ismak ey? What is your name?' I repeated it two or three times. I'm scaring the crap out of this guy, so I made an effort to calm myself and talk in a normal voice. He is begging me not to kill him. 'Only milk, only milk!' he kept crying. That's when I realized he was out risking his life to get some milk for his kids. And that's when my war attitude began to change."

The only sound I hear is Mimi's breath, and then she asks, "What happened then, with the guy and the milk?"

"I escorted him home. His name was Ammar, which means virtuous or pious."

"You mean as an escort so he wouldn't get shot?"

"Yes. But also, that was when I ended my career as a soldier. I removed my helmet and my backpack and went home with him. I stayed with him and his family for two days. On the way to his home, I pulled out a box of Sugar Wafers and shared it with him and we talked about how they were surviving the invasion. He told about his family and said no one in this area of Baghdad was terrorists. I was surprised to find many locals sitting outside their apartments under the shade of awnings. Others were milling about in darkened doorways. A few Iraqis glared at me suspiciously, happy that their friend and neighbor had captured an American Marine."

"Tim, this is a weird story."

"No, it was beautiful, and I felt totally at peace. This man took me to Sanir, his tribal leader, who would take me under his wing, and introduce me to the people we were shooting at. He spoke English but was more shocked when I spoke to him in Arabic. He thought I was nuts to be in this neighborhood alone, but I told him I was sick of the killing and came to him in peace. The next morning, we were with his neighbors and relatives at an outdoor table in an open plaza having tea when a small group of armed fighters entered from a nearby street. They walked cautiously toward us surrounded by a dozen kids dancing and laughing, telling them they had an American.

The leader was a tough-looking young guy named, Hassan, who stepped up to me and studied me menacingly. He was carrying an AK-47 with a belt filled with high-velocity bullets which made me a bit nervous. Hassan turned to Sanir and snarled that I was an invader who had killed many of their people for no reason.

Sanir agreed that his words were true, that many had died protecting this dry and dusty corner of heaven. Then he rose and placed his arms around Hassan's shoulder and told him that on that day, no one shall be killed. Also, as his father's eldest brother, he must obey his orders and put down his weapons. Sanir spread his arms and announced, "Join us for at least one day of peace!"

Hassan asked me why the Americans were shooting at them because they were fighting the same enemy—the people who flew jets into the American buildings!

Mimi, this is the cool part. I gave him the most honest answer I could—straight from the heart. I said in his language that I would tell my officers what I had seen, that I had met an ally who was filled with kindness and a people who only wanted peace. It was like a dam burst. Everyone began laughing and dancing and at first, I thought it was because of my naive remark. But they were ecstatic like a great weight had been lifted, and that it was possible to become allies with the Americans. I went back to the base and told my Captain the entire story. But instead of working with Hassan and his people, he notified me to expect a court martial for deserting my post. He got nowhere with it but I was reprimanded for keeping my unit in the dark about my position. It's not like it's uncommon to lose touch with the base—it's a war zone. As I waited for the court-martial, which takes about a month, I loaded up an ATV with milk, flour, beans, and whatever else I could afford, and delivered it all to Sanir and his people. During my time with them, there were no attacks on any American troops in that part of Baghdad. But it all ended one day when Sanir told me he was worried about my safety because they had spotted Al Qaeda nearby and thought it was a good time to return to my unit."

During my story, I see Mimi sit up and wrap her arms around her knees, quietly staring out the window.

"You stopped the fighting," she says softly.

"Yeah, but only for a brief time, and only in that section of Baghdad. Everyone wants peace but all it took was the killing of the Blackwater guys to get everyone to start shooting again."

"Did the Marines find out about your visits?" asks Mimi.

"Some civilian guys from supply and the commissary ratted me out. They were stealing shit and thought all my big purchases would create suspicion which wouldn't be good for them. My CO got pissed off and threatened me with another court-martial for aiding and abetting the enemy. One day he cornered me and said what he wanted was to put me in front of a firing squad, but I couldn't care less. The hell with him, it was magical."

"Did you have a court martial?"

"Yep. At my trial, I told them what it was all about and that I was using my own money. The military judge decided my actions were foolhardy but not a punishable offense because Sanir was not the enemy. The charges were dismissed to the irritation of my commanding officer, who I think would still like to line me up and shoot me. I might have to go back to Iraq someday if the shit hits the fan again, but it would have to be an emergency. My commander doesn't want me anywhere near him."

Mimi lies back down and kisses me. She has the softest lips.

"You know what, Mimi?" I ask.

"What?"

"It was all worth it for that kiss."

I pull her close and we grow quiet watching the shadows of the leaves and branches outside, rattling and swaying in the wind, dancing across the ceiling.

"There was so much of old Baghdad that looked exactly like it did two thousand years ago—ancient buildings tucked away in a labyrinth of narrow handmade brick streets and alleyways. It was so beautiful, and we were destroying it all to justify the lies of George Bush and the Pentagon. How many centuries have these people, or people like them in the Middle East, been fighting off invaders from the West? This land had remained unchanged since the time of Jesus and we were wiping it off the map.

One day on patrol, I saw a young Iraqi carpenter repairing a storefront and imagined a young Jesus living under Roman occupation and those who fought an invasion from the largest, most powerful military in the world.

I often thought about Hassan and many others and how their experience was so similar to the Roman occupation of Israel. I often thought of the phrase 'what would Jesus do?' Would he be fighting the invaders like Hassan?"

A LONG TIME AGO

After centuries of expansion, wars, and civil strife, the Roman Empire finally settled into a period of economic prosperity and relative peace except for the province of Israel. There were no people in the conquered territories who continued to fight so persistently for freedom as the Jews, which was especially impressive considering their chances of succeeding against the largest army on earth. And it wasn't only the Romans. Herod's successor slew over three thousand Hebrews who had camped outside the Temple demanding freedom. The following year they gathered again and were slaughtered once more.

In the time of the young Jesus, huge slums surrounded Jerusalem and other large cities, which were breeding grounds for zealots who took to the streets regularly, burning the homes and businesses of suspected collaborators.

The roads are lined with the rotting corpses of the recently crucified, while bands of rebels make life dangerous and unsafe, especially for any supporter of Rome. The varied Jewish sects who live in peace in cloistered agricultural communities are also under constant attack and pray for something or someone to ease their suffering—a Messiah to rid them of their enemies and establish the Kingdom of Heaven on earth. Others, with conviction and passion, take matters into their own hands.

Under a bright moon, my friends and I crawl toward our goal through low, dry scrub and rocks until we reach the downhill side

"...a good time would follow, of happiness for the whole world: all earth would be fertile, every seed would bear a thousandfold, wine would be plentiful, poverty would disappear, all men would be healthy and virtuous, and justice, good fellowship, and peace would reign over the earth."

of a flat stone patio the Romans have been using for executions. Once I reached the top, I peer over a low stone wall and see two Roman soldiers guarding three men hanging on substantial wooden crosses, naked, beaten, and bloody, with their arms roped to the cross arms. I am reminded of my brother James' description of our own father's crucifixion and the sadness I felt that has since been replaced by a smoldering anger common among my people.

The soldiers will stand watch until their captain arrives and confirms that all are dead. Unclaimed men will hang here to rot before being removed when a cross is needed for a new round of executions.

We plan to attack the guards when they least expect it, subdue them, and remove those on the cross, dead or alive. Judas would prefer to throw the soldiers over the cliff, but the Romans would kill one hundred of our people if one soldier is harmed. It is best to put a club to the skull—humiliation is rarely reported.

"Watching this scum rot bores me to death," complains one of the soldiers. "Let us find some wine to make the night pass more pleasantly."

"If any discover we have left our post, we will find ourselves hanging up there with them," replies his companion.

The first guard laughs and jabs his spear at a crucified man's chest and gives him a slight poke. With no cry or movement, he laughs, "Who will tell, one of these fellows? You remain here and freeze, but I am off to find something to drink."

His friend looks around the isolated post and the lifeless crucified men, and quickly runs after his companion.

"Hold up! Wait for me!"

They enter a small alleyway, laughing, "Let us raise a cup to the brave Hebrew—toast the scum on their journey to Hades!"

"It is fortunate for them they left," says Judas. "I was looking forward to smashing their skulls."

Once we are certain the soldiers have gone we scramble over the wall. Judas drops a canvas bag to the ground and runs to the alley. His task is to stand guard while we remove the men. I watch him poke his head around the wall into the alley, straining for any sign of movement.

Aaron, John, and I scramble up the steps of the platform and run to the crosses. This is our first attempt to remove the dead at this location which overlooks the city. The view is striking and I understand now why the Romans chose this spot for their brutal display—proclaiming to all that there is no limit to their authority or cruelty. I stop in front of the first crucified man. His skin is a sickly bluish-gray, and his death is certain as a black tongue protrudes from his mouth. Time is not on our side and I must not linger. I remove a rope from the bag and throw it over the cross, then quickly climb up and tie the rope around the man's waist. I cut away the rope from his wrists and lowered him to my friends waiting below.

We quickly wrap him in plain cloth and lower his body over the side. We repeat the same process and remove the second man from the cross who is also dead. As he is lowered into my arms, sadness replaces my anger when I think of my father who must have suffered like this man.

Few remember the child born in Bethlehem so many years ago, then vanished after speaking at the Great Temple in Jerusalem. If you searched for him, which most do not, you would find him tonight in the seaport town of Joppa, stealing Caesar's dead from the crosses.

Judas whistles a warning and we freeze. When he spots the soldiers returning, he acts quickly and runs down the alley toward the guards yelling at the top of his lungs. "Sons of whores! Cuckolds! Your women make love to me while you spend your nights guarding the dead!" He shoves the surprised soldiers against the wall as he runs past, laughing like a madman.

Enraged, the soldiers give chase. We can hear Judas mock them and their slowness. "Death to Rome, the master race of slow, fat pigs!"

We stop our work to run to the wall and watch his progress. From our vantage point, we can see the glow from the guards' torches as they futilely pursue him through the darkened streets.

"Quickly now," I command.

I reach the top of the last cross when suddenly, a bright crack of lightning illuminates the platform, casting an eerie greenish glow on the faces of my friends below. The image sends a chill through my body and I gasp out loud as it reminds me of a dream I once had. It confuses me and I am shaken until the booming of thunder awakens me from my stupor and I clumsily clutch onto the wooden crossbeam.

"Are you alright?" asks Aaron.

I catch my breath and signal yes. I reach out to the crucified man and turn his face toward me, hoping for any sign of life. It would be a miracle if he was, as he was brutally tortured before being dragged through the streets. But the man opens his eyes, surprising me and I lean away in shock, almost losing my grip.

"Bless you," the man whispers. "My prayers...my prayers have been answered." He drops his head onto his chest and I touch his face, which is hot, burning with fever.

"He is alive!" I gleefully shout as quietly as possible.

While we lower the man, again my thoughts are of my father, crucified as he searched for our neighbor, Zacharias, who had been arrested during a violent insurrection. As Zacharias awaited execution, my father traveled to the prison to tell him not to be concerned, and that his family would be cared for after his death. The Romans imprisoned my father too, even though those arrested told them my father was not a part of the riot, and that a mistake had been made. But it made no difference.

How he must have suffered on the cross, and as an innocent man, too. Once again God did not help the pious man who raised the child of Mary, whose birth was told to him by an angel appearing to him in a dream—and some wonder why I have turned elsewhere for inspiration.

It takes all of our strength to lower the bodies down the hillside to the street below where Judas awaits, having lost the soldiers in one of many small narrow alleyways and passages that honeycomb the city. With the living and the dead hoisted upon our shoulders, we cautiously make our way to the safe house of an old freedom fighter.

Saul has spent his life fighting for the zealots, but old age and injuries now find him running a safe house for those fighting the occupation. At this moment, he is sleeping on a pillow-covered chair before a warm fire in the hearth when I knock on his thick wooden door...five quiet knocks so as not to arouse any suspicion from his neighbors. We joke that anything louder might startle him too greatly and stop his heart.

Saul shuffles to the door, then presses his ear against the

door and whispers, "Who goes there so late?"

We give him no answer—only five more quiet knocks.

Saul fumbles with the lock and opens the door. He greets us with a quiet, nervous enthusiasm as he leads us through his home. "Please, please, follow me. Over here, lay him on the bed."

The man is barely alive, moaning in pain from the beating and the hours spent on the cross. I unpack my bag of herbs, and lotions, from my rucksack which I place in a small bowl and mix in warm water with a spoon-shaped alabaster stone until it forms a paste.

"I need hot water," I tell Saul.

Saul wraps a ragged cloth around the handle of an iron kettle hanging over a fire and places it on the floor close to the bed.

I remove the bloodied wrapping carefully, but each time I move the man slightly, he quietly cries out in pain. Even in his condition, he knows not to yell out.

"Soon you will feel nothing," I tell him. A calming tea is brewing and my soothing paste will numb his injuries. When the tea begins working its magic he will find himself asleep, oblivious to his injuries and no longer suffering.

The man has a deep cut on his leg and arm, and I dip a cloth into the kettle of warm water and wash away the dirt thoroughly, then pack it with a clean cloth that I drip honey on which will prevent infection.

"Judas, hold the cloth, tightly."

Judas leans in close and looks at me with a wide grin. It confuses me given the seriousness of the moment until he whispers, "She is a real beauty, that red-haired girl from the estate. I know you think of her constantly, even now while tending to a broken man, she is in your thoughts."

I look up and nearly laugh when I see his twitching eyebrows implying, Right? Right? Am I not right?

I shake my head in feigned disgust and think, how did such an odd creature become my best friend?

"Marry her. You'll never do better," he says.

"Quiet you madman. I need to concentrate on his breathing."

I put my ear to the man's chest and listened. When satisfied that his breathing has returned to normal, I stand back and inspect my work. As there is nothing more to be done, I put away my herbs and oils into my pack.

"He may stay here for as long as it takes to heal," exclaims a grateful Saul. "Strong and brave he is to have survived the torture those brutes put him through."

"The Romans will certainly be looking for him," I say.

"They will not learn of his whereabouts from this house, that I can assure you, young man. God bless you and keep you safe. That was fine work you performed."

I agree that no rumors will leak from his house or this neighborhood. As pressed upon as we are, we are all family, and none would testify against their brother or sister.

After thanking Saul for his hospitality, I step outside into the night and take in the sweet, fresh air. Hours have passed since we first climbed the hill, but our work is incomplete. We still have two bodies to care for, but carrying two bodies through the streets and alleys is much safer than one might assume. At this hour, no soldiers will be found on patrol in this area, lest they have a death wish. One of the men is a laborer who has often worked with Aaron on road-building projects. It is a short but heartbreaking journey to the man's home, and it takes all of our strength not to break down, to weep and mourn when we deliver him to his family. But we must continue—his companion in death, a man with no family, will be taken to the tombs for the poor.

A cool wind hits me in the face as our solemn parade slowly makes its way through the streets. Despite the late hours, I am surprised that we are met by many of the slum's residents outside of their torch-lit homes offering prayers. I suspect that Judas, once free of the guards must have told someone of his exploits on his way back to us and word quickly spread.

An elderly woman wails mournfully for the son of a mother she never knew—maybe her son's life had been taken in our never-ending war against the invader. We journey down a path to the communal burial caves where we are greeted by an old man with a torch at the entrance. He guides us through a maze of tunnels carved out of the rock, and even at this time of night, many mourners can be seen praying and weeping for their departed loved ones. The cave is illuminated by oil lamps hanging on the rock walls to light the cramped passageway, and finally, the old man stops in front of a small, roughly dug alcove. He stands by patiently as we lay our man into the nook and pray silently for deliverance. When our offering is complete, I remove a few coins from my purse and pay the old man for his service.

Arriving at the mouth of the cave, a light rush of wind brings us some needed fresh air. Word has spread of the Roman's latest executions and we are met by hundreds of angry slum dwellers who have filled the road carrying torches and clubs. The crucifixions might be what many say is, "the straw that breaks the camel's back."

We are bumped and jostled and pushed along almost against our will as the agitated crowd chants, "Death to the Infidel! Death to the Romans!" Finally breaking free of the mob, I pull Judas aside and ask if he told anyone of tonight's exploits.

"I might have mentioned to a few friends of my run through the city after taunting the guards," he says sheepishly.

A quiet morning in the Roman garrison's sparsely furnished barracks erupts in fury when a Roman Centurion escorted by an entourage of junior officers pushes their way through the room to the bed of a sleeping soldier.

The Centurion kicks the bed over and spills the soldier onto the floor who then quickly jumps to attention.

Speaking quietly yet forcefully, the Centurion addresses the soldier. "Are you the miserable pile of horse dung left in charge of guarding last night's crucified?"

"Yes, myself and Quintas."

The Centurion steps in close, his face is within inches of the nervous soldier and his voice is severe and threatening. "What is your name, soldier?"

"Gaius, sir!"

"Well, Gaius Sir, did you happen to notice anything missing when you left your post?"

"Anything missing?"

The Centurion strikes Gaius on the side of the head with his fist and knocks him to the ground once more.

Gaius jumps to his feet and stands at attention while bracing for another blow.

The Centurion's face is flushed brilliant red as he screams at Gaius, "You and your worthless friend get out of my sight before I pull your liver out with my bare hands! You find the bastards who are responsible for stealing the emperor's property. Do not dare to return empty-handed! Do you understand!"

"Yes sir!"

"Get your ass moving!"

The Centurion watches Gaius race about putting on most of his uniform and carrying the rest in his arms as he flees the room. As he runs away, the enraged Centurion picks up a small wooden chair and throws it at the departing Gaius, then turns to his entourage and growls, "No terrorist scum lives while I run this company! Is that understood?"

The late morning sun fills my room with a blinding light, and I groan and roll onto my side, but try as I might I cannot force my eyes to remain shut. Still, it is a pleasant feeling to enjoy a few moments more rest. I roll over onto my back and study the plaster walls and rough wood beams of my room as I review last night's rescue. I find my heart is still racing from the adventure, which only ended a few hours ago.

Loud drumming from the Roman barracks startles me. There must be an emergency to call the entire garrison to order. Maybe it is the disappearance of three men from the crosses. They are the property of Rome after all, or at least until official notice is granted to the families to retrieve the bodies. The Roman governor would rather see the corpses rot to be eaten by carrion or wolves, but even they bend occasionally to keep the peace. But a show of force is required lest this insult gives hope to the Hebrews and grows into something larger and more dangerous.

I rise from my bed and walk to a water-filled basin to splash my face and chest, and flinch as the cold water hits my body. I look out the window to the town beyond and think of the young woman, Mary, who I first saw only yesterday, but now seems like an eternity ago. She knows who I am, or at least the story of who I am. Mother's stories of my birth have been the source of much suffering, and I'm certain some might still harbor resentment because of the killings in Bethlehem. My father never spoke to me of it, but I do know the deaths of those children haunted him his entire life.

I finish drying and put on a clean shirt. For a brief moment, I stop thinking about Mary to enjoy the non-stop barking of dogs at the drumming. To me it sounds as if they're telling these invaders, over and over, *go home, go home, go home…*

I enter my father's workshop and my tardiness is of little importance. James, my younger brother, is the workshop foreman, and as usual, has everything humming along very efficiently. Even though I am two years his senior, he became much more skilled in the building trade after I was sent to sea with our uncle. My exile was the result of numerous fights and unruly behavior—the truth being that I was unbearable to live with. Even my teachers could not help me temper my anger.

It was not always so. Until the age of twelve years, I was a loving playful child. I worshiped my mother and father, studied religious texts every day, and worked side-by-side with my father as an apprentice. It was when I learned of the tragedy in Bethlehem and the number of children killed because of my birth—a crime so devastating that it crushed any joy in my heart for many years.

So troublesome had I become, that my parents' only option was to remove me from the house. It was the greatest experience of my life, and did not take long before my volatile nature was subdued by the world's greatness and the vastness of the sea.

It was during my time at sea that the Romans murdered my father. Sadly, I was a thousand miles away in Britannia and only heard of his death when our ship returned home. I learned that

James and mother had walked for two days searching for him, only to find him hanging on the cross along with the others. They took his body from the small cross and laid it on their cart for the long, sad trip home.

James buried father's remains on a small hill overlooking our property with this inscription: *Man will be buried in a grave dug by his own son, fulfilling his destiny according to the prophecy. Yet, if that son is the last, who will bury him?*

My thoughts are interrupted when James greets me cheerfully, "Good day to you, brother!"

"It truly is," I reply.

James embraces me in greeting and says quietly, "Any time we can strike a blow against our enemies, it is a great day. The dining room cabinet is ready for installation."

"I will have Judas help me," I reply.

I make my way deeper into the noisy shop, passing a dozen young boys and men removing raw timber from the vendor's carts, before carrying them to the receiving shed. I greet Aaron and John with an embrace and a hand clasp—a dangerous adventure always seals a tight bond among brothers and friends. I greet the other workers, give praise for good work, or make suggestions if needed.

In the corner of the shop is our classroom where we teach the unskilled our trade and give them an income, providing money for clothing, food, and shelter. I watch as a group of new young students listens attentively to a lesson being taught by Judas.

"You have taken accurate measurements of the height of the wall, correct?" asks Judas.

The room grows silent.

Judas stands with his arms crossed staring tight-lipped at the class as no response is given.

"Correct?" he asks again, this time more forcefully..

"Yes!" the students answer without delay.

"Good. But, what about the width? How many support beams will be required if you need one every three cubits? Once you learn that, you will know how much wood you need to cut."

Judas sees me arrive and jokes, " If there is any lumber left, we will sell it to the Romans for their many crosses. Hail Lord! What noble task awaits us this day?"

This is a daily routine for us—hurling insults as only best friends can do.

"You mock the descendants of the House of David you pagan scum?" I respond. "We are kings! I could remove your nose with the snap of my fingers if I choose to!"

I snap my fingers and Judas covers his face and screams. The younger boys laugh until he turns to them and shows them his mad-dog-fighting face. Then he charges them and shouts, "AAHHG! Run, you little dogs!"

The other men have seen this all before and laugh as the boys scatter from their tables, almost tripping over each other as they flee the charging Judas.

It takes a few patient moments for them to calm down and return to their stools. When all has quieted, I call the group to order for the day's assignments.

"Ori, Yaron! Today you work with Judas and me."

Ori is a thin scrappy eleven-year-old, while Yaron is a more muscular sixteen-year-old. Both boys wear simple work clothes, a loose-fitting shirt over their short pants, and well-worn sandals.

We pull our cart filled with wood and tools along the road to the city gate exchanging talk and laughter, and engage in what we call, "cutting-down sessions., "cutting-down sessions." It is a relief from the mind-numbing hard work we do. In the cutting-down, we trade insults, usually about one's physical features or lack of intellect, and the first one to break and challenge his opponent to a fight is the loser. It is a crude form of learning to survive in a world of cut-throat merchants and opportunists. I know the best negotiators and merchants were probably the best cutting-down players as children.

Yaron and Ori especially love mock-fighting with any object resembling a sword. After a year or two of this activity, they have become excellent fighters, and I wonder how they will fare, if or when the time comes to battle an enemy trained to kill.

"Do not turn your back, ever," instructs Judas. "Watch the hands of your enemy to block his blows, but better is a kick to the knee. A straightened leg will snap in two and render him helpless. If you are still over-matched, aim for his vulnerable areas."

"Vulnerable areas?" asks Yaron.

"Kick him hard in the balls!"

Yaron pauses and asks, "What if he still stands?"

Judas replies, "Then my friend, run like the wind!"

We are near the gates and are dwarfed by the enormous stone wall surrounding the city. A long line of merchants, workers, and travelers wait their turn to enter—a daily occurrence we all suffer through—you must arrive early or spend the day watching your business wither in the heat. Today the wait is longer than usual as outgoing merchants are also subjected to a thorough inspection, and that is odd as they are never bothered. Both sides of the road are jammed with anxious vendors concerned that their goods may not make it to the port in time. Traders exporting goods to other lands should be worried that their produce might spoil before they return home.

When a handful of merchants are allowed through, a mad dash of carts, porters, and donkeys race in to fill the void left by the departed carts. Tempers rarely flare to violence, but if they do, the guards will sweep in like a pack of wolves and quickly put an end to any trouble. We manage to jump in front of a slow-moving caravan with over twenty camels laden with rugs, bundles of cloth, wine, goats, poultry, and whatever else they have buried under their colorful tarpaulins. Once inside the gates, the caravan will wait in another long line at the harbor, and unload their goods for export to the far reaches of the Roman Empire. They will sell what they have carried from as far away as Babylon or Persia, and be gone as soon as business is concluded and once their animals have rested. Tomorrow they will pass through these same gates, loaded with goods from our markets, especially our famous olives, almonds, and dates, to be sold at the other end of the route.

Today, two Roman soldiers are taking their time inspecting the wagons and carts, poking and prodding in every corner even more than usual. Off to the side, we notice an overturned cart with its contents scattered about the rocks and dirt. Someone might have battled for a more advantageous position in line and lost. Possibly someone attempted to smuggle in contraband and was arrested. Occasionally, a merchant who is tired of his existence will snap and decide that this life is simply too miserable and it's a good day to end it all by cursing the guards and the Roman Empire.

As we near the inspection I hear the two soldiers speaking in their native Greek tongue. "Gaius, if we do not find a body soon, we should consider fleeing into the desert," grumbles one.

"This is your fault, you ass. Let us take a bite off the chill you said. I thought they were all dead!"

"Of course they were. Who cares if a few dead terrorists

disappear? As if they will return to life and slay us!"

"Ha! I will surely flee to the desert if one of them does!"

It sounds to me as if these two were the soldiers in charge of guarding last night's crucified and left their post. I glance toward Judas and see a wide smile on his face which tells me my guess is correct. He would be smiling even more if he understood what they were saying. We waited for our turn to be inspected, and maybe we paused too long gawking at the overturned cart. In simple Hebrew the soldier barks at us.

"Move it you, nothing to look at."

Ori, knowing the soldier will not understand him, whispers to Yaron jokingly, "Someone must not have paid the bribe."

The soldier, who is a fierce-looking fellow, spins on his heels and gives Ori a deadly stare.

"Quiet!" I order Ori.

The soldier steps close to me and snarls, "Is there a problem? Do you not like the fine roads and sewage pipes we have built for you complaining bastards?"

I speak to him in Greek, his language, which might have been a mistake. Many lower-ranked soldiers do not appreciate a Hebrew speaking their tongue. After having conquered us many consider it an offense for a Jew to put on any pretense of equality, so I talk to him crudely. "There...no problem. What...happened?"

"He tried to flee the inspection, what does it look like? " he answers quickly before realizing I am speaking Greek. "Where did you learn to speak our tongue?"

"I worked with...physician...merchant ship. Teach me Greek."

"A physician you say? Why would an educated man be working as a common laborer? I think you are a liar. Maybe you learned our language in a Roman prison, and maybe I should smack away your young friend's attitude. Find out if you are lying to me."

I think, *Oh, this one is very angry...and dangerous. Let us not provoke him in the slightest if possible.*

The soldier quickly turns his attention to Ori and threatens him. "I have friends who have died protecting you from terrorists and pirates! Show more respect or you'll not be among the living for long!" Then he snarls at me, "You! Tell your friend to watch his mouth or he will lose the head attached to it!"

The other soldier completes his inspection of our goods and waves us on. Once a fair distance from them, I pat Ori on the head and scruff up his hair. He drops his head, embarrassed by his youthful ignorance, and grins at me sheepishly. Best we move along quickly through the city gate. Before we pass into the city, I take a glance over my shoulder and see the soldiers are still glaring at us with distrust. Maybe they recognize Judas, or maybe it is prejudice toward a common laborer speaking their language. Whatever the reasons for their suspicion, I pray they busy themselves with the inspections and forget all about us.

ALWAYS OPEN

After the publicity I received from the Teenage Jesus vandalism, I received requests for commissions and even landed a couple of meetings with art galleries. Plus, I still have my museum exhibit coming up in a few months, so it's good to give thanks to the unexplainable forces at work in the universe who occasionally show up at the right time. "Thank you, Teenage Jesus."

Despite the favorable opinions from critics and the large public turnout, the attention also brought out some who would like to beat the crap out of me or even kill me if it wasn't against their religion or the law. I've received dozens of angry letters but also got some well-meaning people who said they would pray that I find Jesus before it's too late.

Not all letters expressed outrage. A dozen or so expressed intellectual interest in the subject, such as one open-minded man of God in Kentucky. Also, a woman who taught teenage girls Bible study classes at her church in Tennessee remarked how the picture of a teenage Jesus brought about an interesting discussion, as many of the girls had never thought about Jesus as an attractive and sexual being.

Today, I am sitting on a bench underneath a stand of giant redwoods in our local park. The popular green space is quiet and empty, even more so than usual. The many species of birds who always seem to be in a constant state of battle over food, territory, or mating rituals have also gone still. It's as if there is nothing to complain about, so I close my eyes, feel the warmth and fresh air,

"Jesus, The Teenage Years" is very modern and fresh. I think one of the many things that I enjoy about it, is the way it presents Jesus to a modern audience. It is not unlike images of Jesus, Mary, the Prophets, and Saints painted during the Renaissance. If one looks at Renaissance religious art one will realize that they are all clad in, what was for them, modern apparel. It is shades of a visual Good News Bible, in that it puts images into a modern perspective, one that is immediately recognizable to a fresh new audience.

–Rev. George Bremerton,

Lexington, Kentucky

and think about the sun and the plants. In this moment, one has to appreciate whoever is in charge of life and landscaping.

I've heard quite enough from the angry, holier-than-thou, letter writers. True, I did take some liberties with the painting's characters, but if they had complaints, they didn't get the narrative. Instead, they let dogma rule their emotions.

I was curious why the vandals didn't paint "blasphemy" on the painting, which means an act or offense of speaking sacrilegiously about God or sacred things. Instead, they painted the word "Heresy." Whether they knew it or not, heresy is an opinion profoundly at odds with what is generally accepted. It's also the crime Jesus was crucified for.

I stand up and stretch before continuing my walk. My left shoe feels loose and I notice my shoelace has become untied. As I bend down to tie the lace, I hear a loud "crack," or maybe it's a "thunk" coming from the tree nearest me. On most days I wouldn't have noticed, but today has been unusually quiet. I stand up and look around for the source of the noise, thinking maybe a branch has fallen or a bird broke off a small twig for its nest; who knows? Nothing seems to be out of the ordinary, except for a thrashing noise in a nearby bush and I think, It's probably a rabbit.

This guy doesn't even know what a sinner he is. Next stop buddy, hell. And then you'll come to know how the Lord deals with sinners like you."

Holly is hiding in the bushes just off the trail, having followed the artist five times in the past two weeks, and is now patiently waiting for his scheduled appearance. She knows he'll take the same trail through the park and stop at the same spot to gawk at some giant trees. Earlier in the week she found a secure spot behind a sturdy bush to set up her shot.

The artist stops where Holly knew he would and stares at a large stand of magnificent redwood trees.

Holly can't help but marvel at the incredibly beautiful trees too. There's nothing like them where she was raised, but here they are, smack dab in the middle of a large city, waiting for everyone to notice a prime example of God's great creations. And it is at that very moment that Holly is struck by a blinding flash of light. Her head explodes in pain, her hands begin shaking, and her eyes tear up, making it difficult to focus.

A voice in her head that screams "No, Holly! This is wrong!"

She blinks the tears from her eyes to find the light in her head now hovering over the artist as a glowing, heavenly Angel radiating light like a supernova explosion.

So stunned is she by this event, Holly accidentally pulls the trigger and sets the arrow in flight—straight at the artist's head, until the last moment when the Angel gently pushes the artist over at the waist and the arrow sails harmlessly over his head and sticks into the trunk of a redwood tree.

Holly watches in horror as the Angel turns to her with a look of fury and races toward her with its wings raised, preparing to beat her to death with them. She tosses the crossbow aside and takes flight down the hill, sliding and scrambling through the brush until her foot catches an exposed tree root and she tumbles head-over-heels out of control, narrowly missing a large tree trunk. Holly finally comes to an abrupt halt at the bottom of the hill when she slams into the side of a car sitting in the parking lot.

Wrapped in a brightly colored beach towel, wedged into a

fetal position in the bucket seat of his sports car, Evan slowly begins to wake up. He's confused but not surprised to find himself in the front seat of his car because he was out drinking late into the night. He rubs his temples in a circular motion and yawns while taking a long, drowsy look at his surroundings—a parking lot butting up against a steep hillside covered in bushes. He looks up at a redwood forest at the top of the hill and wishes he could appreciate them, but his throat is dry as a bone and his head is pounding.

"God damn it, I need some water," he says out loud.

He stretches like a cat and rolls his shoulders in slow circles to work out the kinks. Pulling over to sleep it off was the right thing to do—a better alternative to running off the road, or into another car. Laughing to himself, "I am a responsible driver after all."

Evan lifts himself over the stick shift, plops down in the driver's seat, and looks into the mirror for a close inspection—not a good look. He shakes his head disapprovingly at the two-day beard growth and the dried saliva at the corners of his mouth. God, what a mess, he thinks. He wipes away the sleep from his eyes before pushing back his thick brown hair with both hands and finally checks himself out in the mirror one last time before putting on a stylish pair of dark sunglasses.

Evan fumbles around in his pockets for the key and places it into the ignition. But the second the engine kicks over, he recoils in surprise when a loud BANG! erupts, and he throws his hands over his face for protection thinking the engine might have exploded.

"Jesus Christ!" he yells.

He uncovers his eyes and looks for smoke pouring out from under the hood, but there isn't any. Evan listens to the engine and it's still purring like a kitten, then turns around thinking someone has run their car into him. There's nobody in the lot but him and he asks himself, "What the hell?"

Even gets out of the car and looks around at the empty parking lot, looks at the driver's side tires and they're fine. He walks to the front of the car and squats down in front of the grill to smell the engine compartment for a burning oil odor, but everything seems to be normal. Finally, he walks to inspect the passenger side tires and discovers two legs and a body curled up under his car. "Holy shit!" he exclaims and kneels and begins poking an unconscious young woman with his finger—hoping she's alive.

Thankfully the girl emits a quiet moan and Evan gently pulls her out from under the car until she is lying flat on her back on the pavement. He inspects her face, which appears to be uninjured except for a few minor scratches. When he's brushing a bit of dirt from her cheek, he can't help but notice how pretty she is. Evan moves her neck slightly looking for any signs of injury, such as twitching, or sharp movements that might indicate some area of pain. Finally, Evan places his hand under the girl's neck before placing his ear on her chest to listen to her heartbeat.

At that moment, Holly opens her eyes and then gasps in shock to find a man nearly lying on top of her. "Get off me!" she screams and violently pushes the man away and rolls over onto her stomach and frantically looks around at her surroundings.

Knocked to his butt, Evan holds out both hands in surrender. "Hey! Hold on. You just slammed into my car and you might be hurt. Just keep still for a minute, will ya?"

The girl points up the hill beyond the bushes and trees and asks him, "Did you see anything up there?"

"No, I was asleep." He touches her shoulder and tries to calm her. "You're safe now, okay? But you might be injured or in shock, so you need to be still. Can you do that for me?"

Holly quiets and eyes the man suspiciously. "Who are you"

"My name is Evan. What's yours?"

"Holly."

"Okay, Holly, how do you feel?"

Holly rolls her head from side to side. "I think I'm all right."

"Can you sit up?" asks Evan.

Evan holds Holly at the small of her back and helps her to a sitting position.

"Thanks. Are you a doctor?"

"A paramedic, or almost one, I'm still putting in my hours."

Holly pulls her legs to her chest and drops her head to her knees as she begins to cry, "I've done something so wrong. Dear Lord, please forgive me. I have seen your warning and I repent. Please forgive me."

Evan can do nothing at the moment but watch Holly blubber incoherently. Maybe if he asked her a few more questions he might get her to stop crying because something is not right with this chick. "So, what happened up there that had you running into my car? Jesus Christ, you scared the shit out of me!"

Holly turns to Evan with a scowl. "Do not speak the Lord's name in vain." She stares at Evan's rumpled shirt, unkempt hair, and morning growth of whiskers, and asks, "Were you sleeping in your car?"

"Yeah. I think I had too much to drink last night."

"You think? You smell like a bar...or a bum."

"Thank you very much," replies Evan. "That's a nice thing to say to someone who's trying to help you. I guess the patient's acute sense of smell indicates no brain injury."

Holly stares at Evan, puzzled, and asks, "What does smell

have to do with anything? You've been drinking and you smell like liquor."

"It's called, Anosmia. It's a loss of smell from a brain injury."

"I'm sorry," apologizes Holly. "I didn't mean to insult you. I just meant, you know, you look like you slept in your car."

"You didn't answer my question. Why did you run into my car? Was somebody chasing you?"

Color drains from Holly's face and she looks fearfully up the hill, recalling the frightening apparition of the Angel, and dreading the possibility of another sudden appearance. "Something came at me and, I...I guess I got scared."

Holly covers her face with her hands. "How could I have been so wrong?" she cries. "I beg forgiveness. I have sinned against you."

Evan pats Holly on the shoulder to calm her. "Were you with someone? Why were you being chased? And, what were you doing that was so wrong?"

"You wouldn't understand," cries Holly. "I'm a soldier and I've been misled by a false Prophet. I don't know if I will ever be able to atone for my sins."

Evan is now completely bewildered. "I don't know what the hell you're talking about. You're a soldier? Were you in Iraq or something?"

Holly grabs onto the door handle and pulls herself up to stand. She swats at her jeans and sweatshirt knocking off dust and looking around anxiously at the empty parking lot.

"I need to go," she says.

Evan gently takes hold of her arm. "Wait a minute, please. Do you have a car parked somewhere? Because you shouldn't be driving. Let me drive you home...or maybe to an emergency room. Don't take this wrong, but you're acting a little weird."

Holly falls to her knees and begins crying again.

Evan kneels alongside her and puts his arm around her shoulder. "Come on now, how serious could it be? You're alive and it's a beautiful morning. You've met a kind stranger who only wants to help you. How about if we get some breakfast? My treat and you can tell me all about it."

Holly wraps her arms around Evan's waist and hugs him tightly. It calms her until she recalls Reverend Cranston's words about sin and lust, and she quickly pulls away. "I don't consort with non-believers," she snaps.

Evan laughs, "Consort? What century are we in? Look, I believe you're a serious Christian, but, even Jesus consorted with undesirables, and I'm nowhere near as bad as some of those guys. Come on, you can trust me. I am a good guy."

Holly looks down at her scuffed and dirty shoes, then back to Evan who flashes her a charming smile.

"Well...you have come to my aid...and you do seem like a pretty honest person."

"That's the spirit! And we could both use some food, right?"

Evan looks back up the hill. "Did you lose anything up there? I can help you look for it."

Holly ponders the loss of her crossbow for a moment and the reason Reverend Cranston commanded her to use it. "No. There's nothing up there I want anymore."

"Really?" asks Evan. "I could climb up there and get it if it's your purse or something valuable."

Holly stares up at the hillside lost in thought, mostly about the past year and what a fool she's been. "No, let's get out of here."

Evan helps Holly to her feet, taking her arm like a gentleman, and opens the door. She takes a seat in the little sports car and puts on the seat belt before Evan closes the door. With a wide smile, he pats the passenger door, briskly walks around the front of the car, and takes his place behind the wheel. "Ready?" he smiles as he starts the car, then gently races the engine a little to cough out any condensation.

I had the strangest hike this morning—like I was being watched and that's odd because I'm usually not the paranoid type. But you also can't ignore that prickly sensation when the hair on the back of your neck tingles. It's ancient radar from a more dangerous time when not paying attention could get you killed.

I might be a little on edge because of all the wackos who've sent me nasty letters about my art. Thank goodness it's against their religion to kill, but some of them may have found a loophole buried somewhere in their book.

I also need to drink more water because when I stood up after tying my shoe I got a bright flash of light, and that's never happened before. It was a pretty odd sensation that will probably remain unsolved until my doctor tells me I had a stroke or something.

The last portion of my walk features a great view of the ocean uninterrupted by houses, buildings, or trees. While I was looking at the sun begin to rise over the coastal fog bank, I spotted a neat little English sports car below in the parking lot and a young couple who must have gotten up even earlier than me. I smiled when the young man opened the door for the girl and carefully guided her into the seat. He was a real gentleman, something you don't see much of anymore. It was so sweet to watch them.

Evan gets lucky and swoops into the only available parking

spot directly in front of an old-fashioned diner on a busy street. When he's completed his expertly performed parallel parking job, he turns to Holly with a proud smile. Most people don't even know how to do this maneuver without blocking traffic for ten minutes while they make numerous attempts to wedge their car into place.

During their ride, Holly has warmed to Evan's charming ways. He walks around in front of the car to open the door for her, holds out his hand with a smile, and helps her out of the low-sitting vehicle while continuing a conversation they've been engaged in since the park. She playfully laughs at him and his pride over achieving such a simple task.

"Nothing is as bad as a boozer," argues Holly. "I'm from a family of alcoholics, and I'm an alcoholic, too. I stopped drinking a year ago, but I'll always be one."

"I'm sorry to hear that," says Evan. "But I still think your addiction to religion is merely a substitute for alcohol. It's another form of addiction."

"Booze is in your genes and you can't change that. Believing in God has never hurt anyone," replies Holly before her face grows pale when she reminds herself that she just tried to kill a man on the instructions of a so-called holy man who brain-washed her into thinking that carrying out a murder was acceptable. God bless that artist's guardian angel for preventing it from happening and saving her from committing a horrible crime. It's a stain on her soul that she will have to live with for the rest of her life.

Evan notices that Holly has gone quiet in the middle of a conversation. "Are you okay?" he asks.

"Yeah, I'm fine. Just a momentary relapse. Sorry."

Evan continues. "Anyway, despite Jesus' good intentions, many of his followers are responsible for the deaths of a lot of innocent people."

"Don't blame Jesus for man's shortcomings," replies Holly.

"I don't. But when will it end? After two thousand years, we're as pathetic as ever. Let's talk about it inside. I'm starving."

Evan holds the door open for Holly, and he's already noticed how pretty she is even with her scuffed-up denims, her floppy hoodie sweatshirt, and also, she has a nice figure.

"Who knows? Maybe we can help each other," says Evan.

"I'm not sure you'll want to know me once I tell you what my life was like before slamming into your car."

"Why don't we call it divine intervention," laughs Evan. "How bad could it have been anyway? I was passed out in my car."

"I've heard you've got to be sick before you get well," laughs Holly.

The noisy breakfast crowd all turn their heads when the bell over the door rings and interrupts conversation. They immediately make snap judgments about the two scruffy-looking kids at the door before returning to their pancakes and eggs.

The aroma of frying bacon and percolating coffee ends any further talk as Holly and Evan scout out an empty table or booth, but none are available. The irresistible smell of breakfast is making their mouths water, so they decide on two adjoining seats at the counter. The world is tuned out while they become quietly engrossed reading through the menu while visualizing a plate filled with hash browns, fresh eggs, and sausage.

Once he's made his decision, Evan lays down the menu and asks Holly, "Can we hang out after breakfast? Maybe take a drive up the coast and breath in some cool air?"

Holly turns and studies Even—his strong jawline, bright blue eyes, thick brown wavy hair, and a good physique. It takes her a moment to reply when she realizes that this is the first time anyone has asked her for a date since high school. *How pathetic that I let my life drop so low,* she thinks. "I would love to. You know, I haven't even left the city since I arrived."

Holly and Evan turn their heads in unison when a patron calls out to the waitress and the usual patrons as he leaves, "See you tomorrow!" The door's bell rings when he opens the door and the clamor from the busy street rushes in, only ending when the door closes.

Both Holly and Evan take notice of the sign on the glass door in red lettering that reads, "Always Open," and turn to each other in surprise.

Evan nods his head and chuckles, "True enough."

"That's a rule I'm gonna live by," says Holly.

HONORABLE DISCHARGE

A deep restful sleep ends quickly when Holly is jolted awake by her cell phone chiming *Imagine* by John Lennon. The name on the screen informs her that her career as a Watchman is nearly at an end.

She picks up the phone and answers matter-of-factly, "Hello."

There's a long pause before the caller speaks. "Am I still the Father, Sister Holly?"

Holly can hear it in his voice, the pitch an octave higher than usual and full of tension. The Honorable Reverend Eugene Cranston is furious and Holly knows why, but she doesn't answer him.

"Were my orders unclear to you?"

"No," responds Holly quietly but confidentially.

"Explain to me why you chose to ignore my instructions."

Holly doesn't have the words to describe what happened in the park. All she can do is tell Reverend Cranston the truth. "What you asked of me was a terrible thing and an unholy act. That artist is protected by God, I saw it!"

Holly waits for a response, but Reverend Cranston and the phone goes silent.

The centerpiece in Reverend Cranston's sparsely furnished wood-paneled room is a framed painting of a fair-skinned, golden blond-haired Jesus hanging on the wall above his desk observing every move and word spoken from a distant heaven. The reverend knows He is everywhere and in everything, and at this moment he knows his savior is not pleased.

Reverend Cranston holds the phone away from his ear and stares at it dumbfounded. "Yes dear child, the Scriptures are wrong. The scribes who translated the words of the prophets are liars. God himself is untruthful. But a sinful, lowly creature like yourself has decided that only she possesses the truth. Is that what you are telling me, Sister Holly?"

"You weren't there, but I know what I saw. That artist has a protector, an angel more powerful than you can imagine. Because of what I was about to do, it came at me, lifted me off my feet, and tossed me down a hill!"

"I see," says Reverend Cranston. "This agent of Satan has a powerful guardian angel, but you, a believer in the teachings of Jesus Christ do not. Does that make any sense?"

"You're good at confusing people reverend, but I know, and just in time, that what I was doing was wrong."

Reverend Cranston tries to calm his voice in an attempt to soothe his warrior. "What you saw was a horrible vision, Sister. I understand, but how do I counsel one who has no wisdom?"

"It was not a horrible vision! " cries Holly. "It was real...and frightening...and it was beautiful too."

Reverend Cranston turns and looks to his painting of Jesus hoping to gain the strength he'll need to bring his warrior back to him and the church. "Satan can take many forms. Maybe what you saw was not an angel at all, but Satan himself. Satan is a trickster and a shape-changer. Many have been drawn into his smooth talk and false promises."

Holly screams into the phone, "You're not listening to me! A miracle happened, don}t you get it! And all you care about is your end-of-the-world agenda. Don't you see? I received a message, a message from God!"

Reverend Cranston kneels in prayer. "Pray with me, Sister. Get down on your knees with me and pray for wisdom and salvation." He closes his eyes and reaches his hands skyward. "Vindicate me, oh God, and plead my cause against an ungodly nation; oh deliver me from deceitful and unjust man!"

Holly interrupts the reverend abruptly. "I won't pray with you Eugene, not anymore."

Reverend Cranston grabs the phone off the desk and slams it up against his mouth. "Now you listen to me, little girl. Disobedience will be dealt with most harshly. Do you understand me?"

Holly yells into the phone while throwing her few belongings onto the bed. "No! You listen to me! There are people—loving, caring human beings whose only sin is that they don't fit into your way of thinking. You took advantage of me. You almost made me kill a man! Well, not anymore. I'm free for the first time in years and I'm taking back my life! I've seen the light, Eugene, and what I now know as truth is not what you preach."

Reverend Cranston has one threat left in his arsenal of Biblical rantings, his go-to warning that always works on the gullible who have lost their faith. "The end is near Sister Holly. Do you truly feel this is a good time to fall from grace? Such a short time is left to us before the Sixth Angel trumpets the Rapture, but I cannot save your soul from an eternity of pain and fire if you embark on this sinful course."

With her clothes folded and tucked into the backpack, Holly zips it up and tells the Cranston, "You sent me to kill a man whose only sin, in your mind, was that he painted a picture of a young

Jesus. You are the one who is on his way to Hell! Repent for your sins, Reverend, you're going to need to!"

Reverend Cranston explodes. "Whore! Heretic! Blasphemer! The punishment of the iniquity of the daughter of my people is greater than the punishment of the sin of Sodom. There is no hand to help her! Lamentations 3-4. Damn you to...."

"Go to Hell," says Holly quietly and hangs up on him. She takes a moment to stare at the phone and thinks about what she's just done, and how good it makes her feel. She's free from Eugene's grip, the lying charlatan that convinced her to be a soldier for God. But, and even better, she's just met a nice boy who made her laugh even over the dumbest stuff, and feel joyful for the first time in an eternity,.

Holly stares at the small poster of that Teenage Jesus painting and beams a wide smile as she thinks, *all this fuss over some art.* She thinks about the path she traveled to destroy it, then orders to kill the man who created it. "Brainwashed," she says out loud.

Holly walks to the small bathroom and turns on the sink faucet. She watches the water slowly fill the basin, then dunks her head under the water and holds it there for as long as possible. Thirty seconds later and out of breath, she lifts her head gasping for air, then plops down on the floor crying and laughing at the same time, her heart filled with joy. With water and tears dripping down the front of her shirt, she covers her face with cupped hands and prays, "You drew me near and You said do not fear any longer. Thank you. You have redeemed my soul, and I am free."

Before she leaves the hotel room, Holly tears the Jesus poster off the wall, folds it up and shoves it into the back pocket of her jeans. *Might as well have a reference point,* she thinks.

THE MISSING YEARS

Today I am installing elaborate brass handles for the cabinet drawers of a large buffet in the dining hall. The splashing of water in the pool below and the childish high-pitched laughter of Joseph's two children, Simon and Martha, echo throughout the room and it makes me think, of being a child again playing in Joseph's pool—living for the moment when life was simple and free from worry.

My thoughts vanish when I hear Mary's voice telling the children to pay attention to the lesson. She is all I have thought about for the past three days and has me putting down my tool and walking to the balcony.

From my perch, I watch Joseph's children excitedly splash about while Mary and her handmaiden attempt to teach them how to swim. The children hold on to the tiled edge kicking their feet and squealing with delight as they pretend a sea serpent is chasing them.

"Pay attention now and watch me," says Mary as she pushes away from the pool's edge and begins a leisurely but very advanced underwater stroke. Upon reaching the surface she turns gracefully onto her back with her eyes closed, effortlessly floating without the slightest movement of her arms. But what I notice most, much more than the expert swimming technique, is her long red hair enveloping her body over her swimming costume.

Mary blinks the water out of her eyes and spots me on the balcony watching her—and she does not turn away.

As much as I should avert my eyes, I cannot.

Joseph enters without a sound, and I am startled when I hear his voice just over my shoulder. "She certainly is beautiful."

I turn to him with a dumb grin and stutter like an idiot, "Oh, oh, yes…yes she is."

He nods and says, "Everyone loves her it seems, especially my wife. And the children cannot receive enough of her attention. The workers too, seem to find her presence a benefit."

I am certain he is referring to me, and I am ashamed my behavior is so disrespectful toward my uncle's hospitality. I feel like climbing under a rock. "Forgive me, please. I did not mean to be looking at Mary."

"Jesus my son, I take no offense. There is nothing you can do to make me angry with you. I do not know if you are aware of it, but Mary has spoken to my wife about you. She asks many questions also, and pray tell…I have no idea why. Do you?

My uncle is toying with me, of course, but this news comes as a surprise. Her interest in me is very encouraging.

Joseph continues. "Did you know that Mary works with the poor, much like yourself? I wish I could assist her in more ways, but the priests and the governor complain that already I give too much of my wealth to the poor. The cowards fear I might become too influential and threaten their grip on power. We must be careful or they will make life difficult for all of us."

"How is it that we are unable to overcome such lunacy?"

"That is the way of politics, son. Our king is ruled by Rome, which keeps us all walking on a tightrope. Mary also has her own ways of finding provisions for her work, and to assist in this, I ask many merchants to give her a helping hand. Please, do not tell her I told you this. She is a very proud young woman."

"What kind of work requires your help this?" I ask.

"Mary and her maid load up the wagon nearly every morning and drive into the worst parts of the city. She is using her wealth to enrich the lives of others. I am surprised you have not seen her. It is quite remarkable."

Joseph looks about the room. "I must attend to business. Work is progressing nicely."

"Thank you. It should be completed soon."

"That is good to hear," he laughs. "My wife is ready to divorce me because of the dust and constant noise. My only defense is that it was her idea in the first place to enlarge the villa."

The children see us and call out from below, "Jesus! Jesus! Come here! Swim with us!"

"I am working," I answer.

"Please!" the children yell in unison.

Mary joins in the chorus. "Yes, please join us. You can help me dry them off!"

Joseph nudges me. "Go help our Mary. You should take more time away from this construction. I insist, go enjoy yourself."

I shrug my shoulders "Why not" and make my way outside to the pool. Mary swims to the water's edge and watches me while I take off my sandals and sit on the edge of a cushioned lounge.

"Dry me off first!" demands Simon.

I quickly grab a towel lying on the couch and snap it at the ground. "Which one of you goes first?" I laugh.

The children cry in surprise at the loud sound and lose their enthusiasm immediately. Martha cries, "Take him!"

"I will go first, then," says Simon. "I am brave and she is not!"

"Remember your manners and always let the ladies go first."

Martha climbs out of the pool with a squeal of delight and I dry her off and wrap her in the towel. She sits next to me on the couch and leans her head against my side.

Mary's girl calls out from a room adjacent to the pool. "Finish drying off and prepare for afternoon lessons!"

The children complain briefly and walk sullenly to the house. "It is not fair!" whines Simon. "Even slaves tell me what to do!"

"Simon!" chastises Mary. "Sarah is our companion and your teacher. Please behave yourself and show her respect!"

"I'm sorry," he moans.

Mary climbs from the pool and wraps a large towel around herself. I watch her as she whisks water from her hair and then ties it with a leather strap she picks up from the pool's edge. She comes to where I sit and takes her place on the lounge, ignoring me while she dries her legs and feet. A sly smile on her face tells me she knows I am watching her and she seems to be enjoying my discomfort.

I wait for a moment before finally turning to her and saying, "I must apologize. I was gazing at you while you were swimming."

Mary lets my apology hang in the air while she continues to dry off. "You mean when I was partially dressed?"

I almost cough in surprise at her plain-speaking comment.

"Why do you feel a need to apologize?" she asks.

I shake my head. "I cannot think as the Roman, nor a young woman from Syria."

Mary asks, "I wonder, are we so different?"

"Ancient laws govern our hearts," I reply.

"Who then has taught us to ignore what the heart feels?"

"That is man's lesson, given to us by the Prophets."

"But the Prophets are only men. Did they not learn the

lessons of the heart?" she asks.

Having spent my entire childhood engulfed in religious studies, I reply, "The word of the Torah is the word of God. But, you are correct in asking why should not the heart rule over dogma instead of the opposite. There is an ancient saying; 'truth is beauty.' All my life I have believed that beauty comes from within."

Mary replies with a sly smile. "Then the God who created us must be within, correct? If you respond to beauty, which is truth as you say, then why do you feel shame?"

I wonder, is she testing my faith, teasing me, or both?

"Our culture has imprinted emotions and behavior which dictates how we unconsciously respond to stimulus. Laws and codes of behavior have been made necessary to survive as a people. Maybe in these modern times, some of the stories and rules seem a bit harsh, maybe even foolish, but our culture has created who we are. I still feel I owe you an apology for staring at you."

"You are very thoughtful, which is a very attractive quality." laughs Mary. "But see how comfortable you are with me now even though I am still only wrapped in a swimming costume."

"It seems our conversation has put me at ease."

"Did you gaze at me because you found me attractive?"

How is it that women, the so-called weaker sex, can enslave the strongest man with a simple word or a flirtatious look? If that is her game, we men have our weapons also, the truth.

"Yes, you are very beautiful," I reply confidently.

Mary is caught off guard and flinches. Maybe she was expecting a more cautious answer. But then, just as quickly, she lifts her head and smiles so tenderly that my face flushes. "And you are too confident," she laughs. "But, thank you for saying it."

While we listen to the water lapping against the mosaic-tiled edges of the pool built by Hebrews, I think of the soldiers who inspected our cart the other day, boasting of Roman architecture and engineering. I wanted to ask him who he thought built all their magnificent roads and buildings. My reward for giving that man a history lesson would end up with a crack to the skull from his baton.

Mary ends our quiet moment when she asks, "You and your friend Judas seem very close, almost like brothers. How is it that you come to know someone like him?"

"If you are saying you think he looks like a criminal, you are correct. The first time we met, I was a young boy and he robbed me. I fought him off but he was much bigger than I and took my purse."

"Did you ever get your money back?"

"No. I never did. But he thought my struggle against him to be so comical, he began looking out for me. We have been friends ever since although he might still slap me on the head if I act the fool, feeling I deserved to be taught a good lesson."

"What a horrible friend!"

"Mary, he was an orphan and lived on the streets his entire young life. My family was an easy target for him because we had some wealth even though that is no excuse for thievery. Shortly after being robbed, my father told me to point out the boy who stole from me. Once I did, Joseph told me to go home and let him talk to Judas alone. I thought my father might thrash him, but instead, he gave Judas a job as an apprentice builder. As it turned out, Judas was very good with numbers and he became our estimator."

"And that was the end of his thievery?"

"He never stole from us again. Judas has a heart of gold once you earn his respect. To meet him is to dislike him; to know him is to love him."

Mary has a quizzical look on her face like I must be mad for having this man as my closest companion.

"If you love him, then I will learn to love him too."

Now it is my turn to have a puzzled look of surprise.

Sarah calls out from the pool house that the children are ready for the afternoon's lessons. I rise from the lounge while Mary gathers up her sandals and offer her my hand. She receives it with such grace that it startles me, and I think, how can such a brief touch reveal so much? The sensation of her soft smooth skin and warmth. I also wonder what she feels holding my rough calloused hands.

Before she enters the pool house, she stops and turns to me with a smile, a look that invites me to pursue our friendship.

I take my time putting on my sandals and imagining a life with a woman like her. Before I return to work, I look to the balcony from where I first sighted her swimming and savor the memory.

The walk to the unfinished cabinet is a slow one. I am filled with many conflicting thoughts concerning the relationship between a man and a woman. We have so many laws, both civil and religious, that dictate how we must think and feel about the opposite sex. It has been over one thousand years since Moses walked down the mountain with the Ten Commandments, although some believe there were more. It is told that he became angered at his people worshiping a false idol and broke one of the tablets. If it were me, I would not destroy the word of God etched in stone in a fit of anger. It is a wonder that Moses was not punished, either by God or by his own people. Since that time, the scribes and priests have created hundreds of additional commandments, many with differing opinions and interpretations depending on whether you abide by Hillel, a liberal teacher, or the conservative Rabbi

Shammai, who demands a strict interpretation of the Torah.

Today there are over fifty-seven commandments alone regarding incest. The purpose of those is very clear as we are a relatively small tribe. It is important that the marriage contract, which has more to do with creating and protecting wealth, does not occur between a man and woman too closely related.

During my years of study, I often wondered why, in all of these rules and commandments, there is so very little written about the love between a husband and wife. Maybe the pursuit of a desired partner is too fraught with emotion and too difficult to govern. It is so much easier to simply draw up a contract to bind the two and their families.

We are nearing the end of construction on a small house in town for a poor woman and her three children. Their state of poverty resulted in the imprisonment of her husband who was arrested after complaining about the lack of food in the markets. He was forced to defend his position before a corrupt magistrate who jailed him after it was discovered the man had no bribe to offer. Along with the shelter we are building, we have paid the magistrate his money, and her husband will soon be released.

As more Roman citizens emigrate to our land, they do not hesitate to displace many of the original inhabitants from their homes if the land is desirable. Unethical officials find loopholes in land grants to steal farms that have been in the same family for hundreds of years. Many are confiscated for the most transparent of reasons—condemnation for the public good, or need of a new road that is rarely ever built, and the worst being for security reasons. Money collected from taxes fills the treasure chests of the Romans, who pass on a small percentage to Herod, who only cares for glory. For many years, his money has been spent on building the Great Temple in Jerusalem as a tribute to his grandfather's name. Because of this, he has sent the territory into near ruin.

I sit on a block of stone taking a short break from work, and tilt my head back for a long refreshing drink of water from a jug on this warm day. My thoughts and complaints about the evil that is a part of daily life in our land evaporate when I spot Mary and her friend Sarah, driving a cart loaded with goods a few streets away. I quickly put down the jug and picked up my backpack.

"Yaron, come with me."

By the look on his face, he must have seen the girls too, and I think he might have an interest in Sarah. I signal for him to follow me down the rough pathway to the paved street below where Mary's cart has stopped a short distance away where she has already begun unloading goods. By the time we reach them, a line of poor women and children have queued up waiting patiently for the food and clothing the girls are distributing.

We approach without them noticing and stand near the cart watching them work. The line is long but it moves quickly as each woman stops in front of Mary and accepts a caged chicken, a basket of eggs, and a small bundle of cloth. So busy is she that she doesn't notice me at all. Yaron seems only to notice Sarah, who is transfixed by my handsome apprentice turns away, embarrassed I assume, because of their mutual leering.

Mary admonishes Sarah her being foolish in front of the destitute, then follows Sarah's gaze until it lands on Yaron and me. There is such a surprised look on her face that I cannot help but laugh. She recovers quickly and berates us. "Sneaking around the streets frightening unsuspecting women and children are you? Well, now that you're here, maybe you could lend us a hand."

She lifts her chin defiantly and waits for my answer, and I know what I decide to do will be very important if I ever want to see more of this girl. I could give her an honest but weak excuse—I do need to return to work to supervise my crew, or I could tell her that she seems to be doing very well on her own. Instead, I turn and ask, "Yaron, should we help them unload those goods?"

Yaron happily agrees that indeed we should.

Mary orders us to begin sorting through whatever is asked for. We hand the items to Mary or Sarah, who in turn gives each family a bundle of clothing and food.

"God bless you," each one says, and one young mother kisses Mary's hand while giving thanks.

The cart is stacked with a few cages of small animals, mostly chickens and pigeons, and I wonder if she knows that Joseph has been helping her.

"How do you come to own this?" I ask. "It must take much effort and time searching the local farms. How is this possible while you are tutoring Joseph's children also?"

Mary proudly states, "Each morning there is a long line of vendors outside of the synagogue. Most do not enjoy spending the entire morning almost giving away their products to the money-lenders who gouge them terribly. I offer them a fair price."

I gasp. "Those animals are for the money-lenders who buy them for the sacrifice! You are putting yourself in great danger by taking away their profits."

Mary scoffs, "The poor vendors are hardly paid anything by the money changers. After nearly stealing the goods, those foul men turn around and sell the same animals for ten times the money. I pay the vendor much more and the poor receive a goat to milk, or eggs from a chicken."

"The money-lenders will not appreciate an outsider taking away their profits," I reply. "They have many spies and are a very powerful group of men."

"I may not have to *steal* the goods anymore as many merchants now come to me first before going to the Temple. I know some are friends of Joseph, but they know me to be an honest merchant who pays a good price for their products. The money-changers cannot stop the merchants from doing business, can they?"

"Those people can do anything they want," I reply. "They will make false accusations or threats on your life. They can have you arrested for no reason at all. They have done this to many others."

"I have never been concerned for my safety. Let them do what they will, or do what is right and help us with our work."

The money-lenders are not greedy, provincial boys with eyes on her property. They are cold-blooded thieves who will stop any threat to their profits by any means possible. I do not think my pleas will convince Mary to use more caution, so I make a vow to watch over her and keep her from harm.

A young mother with two small children steps forward for her package and I notice one of the children, a small boy, who has a severely infected eye.

"May I inspect his eye?" I ask the mother.

The young mother directs her child to go to me. "I will be by your side," she tells him.

I have seen this condition many times before, especially in poor neighborhoods where unsanitary conditions are made worse by fetid wells. I search through my rucksack for a small glass vile of oil and a packet of herbs, remove a clean cloth, and tear off a small piece. "Come close," I ask the boy and clean the eye with the salve, a mix of herbs and oil. I place the salve on another clean piece of cloth and fold it into a small eye patch.

"Hold this over his eye, please," I instruct the mother, and I rip a length of cloth and wrap it around the child's head, tying it securely to hold the medicinal patch in place. "Keep this over his eye for three days then remove it. After that, add two drops from the vial directly into his eye, once a day."

When the mother kisses my hand as I hand her the vial, I'm embarrassed by the display of affection, but it gives me great satisfaction to be of help.

All of this takes a few moments, and I am so focused on my task that I sometimes lose myself to any events around me. When I have finished with the child, I look up and find Mary, Sarah, and Yaron have stopped handing out goods. Even the poor women stand by silently watching me repair the child's eye.

"That was very impressive," says Mary. "What a surprise to learn my filthy carpenter is also a healer?"

Did she say, My filthy carpenter? I am pleased she is a witness to my true calling, still only a student with much more to learn from others more knowledgeable than I am.

I drop my head and reply, "I know a few techniques taught to me by a man who was truly a gifted healer."

"You know more than a few techniques," she replies.

My healing pales when compared to Mary's work. The energy and effort she gives to strangers...it is she who shines. There is no danger in being a healer. Everyone loves the physician, the one who relieves pain and suffering. It is hard to imagine that feeding the poor should be considered a threat, but it is, especially if that work is a threat to those in power.

Mary reaches for another bundle and inadvertently touches my hand. Instead of recoiling, she takes hold and studies the comparison of the light olive color of her skin to my darker tone. She touches my fingers and turns my hand over and traces her fingers over my palm as if looking at a map. Our eyes meet and we hold our gaze and there are no words to describe what I feel at this moment except to say that my heart is beating rapidly.

A clearing of the throat, or maybe it is a cough that interrupts our moment. Embarrassed, we turn away to face the large number of poor standing in front of us who require attention. Yet, they too are transfixed and appear to have enjoyed our moment of discovery as much as Mary and me.

We return to the work at hand, but I cannot stop worrying about the danger Mary and Sarah will be facing should word spread of their good deeds.

"This work you take on, would you like assistance? Yaron is strong and a very hard worker. Do not worry about paying him; I will take care of that if you do not mind."

Mary turns to Yaron. "Would you like to help us?"

So caught up in my world, I had not considered that others might be falling in love, too. I see that Yaron is infatuated with Sarah, and she is with him. He takes a glance at Sarah, who is smiling brightly at him.

"I would!" he exclaims, maybe a bit too happily, then bows his head in embarrassment and says, "If that is what you want."

"I want you to be watchful at all times. Temple spies are everywhere, and we cannot risk having them arrested. Will you take this task seriously?"

"Yes, I promise," he vows.

Across the square, a man, a known money-changer for the Temple, stands near a priest and observes us. The priest cups his hand over his mouth and says to his companion, "This is unusual as you have reported, but I see only kindness. More of our citizens should be helping one another like these young people."

The money-changer shakes his head in disagreement. "I see treason. Look how they control the masses already. This idealism will one day bring about your destruction. "

"You exaggerate," replies the priest. "These young people have never been a source of trouble. The young man is Jesus, who preached in the temples as a child."

"Yes, I know who he is. Now he is a wealthy builder. I ask you, when did you last hear him preach? I do not trust this young man, and I trust this daughter of the Sadducee even less."

I notice the two men whispering to one another and turn to Mary. "Look, we have important visitors beyond."

Mary takes a glance at the men and quips, "Do they not approve of our work?"

"They are here because they are concerned," I reply.

"Their concern is unnecessary as I am no threat to their power," says Mary.

"What you say is true, but they decide what is a threat or not. Promise me you will tell Yaron if you suspect any trouble."

That same day, my crew and I gathered at a tavern to celebrate the completion of the poor woman's home and to pay the men their wages. Our table is laden with bowls of fruit, dried seasoned meats, and plenty of drink, but the men are behaving strangely; smirking, odd grins, and joking cackles that seem to be directed at me. Is my state of bliss that obvious? They are worse than old hens.

Happiness is often a short-lived affair as nearby a tradesman who has consumed too much wine is directing some of hostile loud and obnoxious comments at me. I hear him slur, "His whore is the daughter of a wealthy man, a collaborator! Filth! Like all those other Sadducees."

His companions try in earnest to quiet his drunken tirade and make an attempt to pull him away, but he breaks their grip. "I could care less if he hears me. Toadying up to those Roman shits, consorting with our enemies."

Unable to tolerate the insults any longer, I go to the man, then place my hand firmly on his shoulder, and tell him, "Listen, you are drunk. Go home to your family before you regret this."

He screams and swipes my arms away. "Get your filthy hands off me! You and your family are scum! Collaborators!"

I squeeze his shoulders hard and tell him forcefully, "Be still! You are acting the fool!"

"Those people of Bethlehem are the fools!"

His words stop me cold and, unable to bear him anymore, I violently throw him to the ground. But even as I walk away from him he continues to curse me. That is the disease of anger, as I return to my friends in worse shape than before. My heart is racing, my hands are trembling, and can only calm myself by taking slow deep breaths.

Judas throws aside his stool and charges the man. He easily lifts him off the ground by his shirt and screams, "You worthless dog! If you utter another word, I will rip your throat out!"

Judas shoves the tradesman away, fortunately for him, too, as he is merely a coward with a big mouth staggering away from the tavern.

Judas returns to us laughing and tries to comfort me. "Do not let that toad get to you. I know that man and he is an idiot who has been beaten down often enough that he should know better."

It has been a humiliating week for the Roman soldiers, Gaius and Quintas, still under orders to locate the missing terrorists removed from Caesar's cross in a bold act of subversion. They've spent days poking their heads into curtain-covered openings of shops hoping to spot a twitch or a stutter from a merchant when asked about the theft of three men on the cross.

Gaius stands at the entrance of an herb shop, waiting for his eyes to grow accustomed to the dark little room.

"May I assist you officer?" asks a voice in the dark.

Gaius grunts and backs out of the store, turning to Quintas and complaining, "I was trained to fight, not search for ghosts. Those men are dead I tell you?"

Quintas replies, "If we do not find a body soon, dead or alive, we might consider fleeing to the desert."

The soldiers cease their grumbling when they hear someone moaning a complaint in a narrow alleyway. They stop and listen for a few moments before noticing a man lying face-up in the alley. The drunk is cursing to himself, "Scum. All of them, a scourge on our land."

Quintas approaches the tradesman with interest and speaks to him in broken Hebrew. "Hey! You! Get up. "

"Lick my balls!" slurs the tradesman.

Quintas places his foot on the tradesman's neck. "What did you say?"

The drunk man struggles, flailing with his fists while trying in vain to hit the legs of Quintas. "Get off me, Roman pig!"

Quintas laughs and presses his weight down on the neck. "Settle down or it will be you who is killed."

Recognizing his struggle is fruitless, the man quickly ceases his fight. When he calms down, Quintas takes his foot off his neck and allows the man to pull himself to his knees gasping for breath. Quintas lifts him off the ground and shoves him against the wall.

"Take it easy!" screams the man.

"You ignorant ass, here is how it is going to be. First, we beat you, then we haul your drunken ass off to prison. There, you will be beaten by others before your dead and broken body is dumped on the street. How does that sound?"

The man begins begging for his life. "Prison? No, wait! I have had too much drink, that is all. Please forgive me! Please!"

Gaius slams the tradesman against the wall. "You called us pigs, you ignorant shit! That demands a sound thrashing. What do you think, Quintas, one hundred lashes?"

"More if the captain is in a foul mood, which he normally is," laughs Quintas.

"Wait! Wait! What glory to arrest a common drunk? I know of others—zealots and revolutionaries. That is who you want. "

"Is that so? Zealots are they?"

Quintas looks at Gaius with a big, open grin. "Then take us to these Zealots you speak of."

"No! No! They would kill me. I am no collaborator!" cries the tradesman.

"No, you are not a collaborator, you are a miserable coward who would say anything to save his skin."

"You must believe me!" wails the tradesman. "I tell the truth. They are working in town as I speak. Judas is the worst of them. Another is called Jesus. They are drinking at a tavern at this moment. They are who you seek, not me, a pitiful lowly mason!"

"Okay lowly tradesman, we will seek out these Zealots. But if you have lied to us, be prepared to die on one of our many fine crosses," growls Gaius.

"Why are we wasting our time on this scum," asks Quintas. "Beating him is too much effort. Setting him afire would be much less trouble."

"No! Please! I tell the truth. They know of others too! Torture them if you must. They are cowards and will talk freely once put to the blade!"

Gaius shoves the tradesman to the ground. "These terrorists at least put up a fight! Get your cowardly ass out of my sight!" Gaius kicks the tradesman in the ribs and laughs when the man screams before jumping to his feet and running out of the alley holding his side.

"Let us seek out these zealots. If he is lying, may his death be a hundredfold more painful than mine," says Gaius.

"Two living terrorists are better than three dead ones. We may live through this after all," replies Quintas.

Gaius and Quintas watch from a recessed entry of a shop across the street from the tavern told to them by the tradesman and watch a dozen young men end their meeting, collect their tools, and part ways.

"Zealots?" asks Gaius, "Or young construction workers; what do you think Quintas?"

"Does it make any difference? Let's find these Judas and Jesus characters; maybe they will talk as easily as that drunk."

They pick two young workers and follow them into a crowded neighborhood. So intent are they stalking their prey they fail to notice many hostile residents crowding into the street.

"What are you looking at? Back to your business," commands Quintas.

Hillel and Eban, slow their pace when they hear bird whistles coming from rooftops—a signal they are being followed and may be in danger. They turn their heads to spot two Roman soldiers following them and decide to lead the two deeper into the ghetto. At a small square, the two young men stop and wait for the soldiers.

Gaius and Quintas approach them aggressively and before asking any questions push them up against the wall. "Which one of you is known as Judas?" demands Gaius.

"We saw you leave the tavern. One of you is Judas!"

"We don't know of any Judas," says Hillel. "Why don't you return to your barracks and sleep off the wine?"

Gaius shoves his baton into Hillel's stomach and he doubles over in pain and falls to his knees.

Gaius turns to Quintas with an evil grin and laughs, "Not bad for a drunk!" He turns his attention back to Hillel. "Do you have something else you want to say?"

Quintas grabs Eban. "What about you? Are you Jesus?"

Eban defiantly responds, "Which Jesus are you looking for? It is a common name around here."

The violent questioning lasts only for a moment before dozens of men emerge from doorways and alleyways. Suddenly, Gaius and Quintas find themselves surrounded by a large number of angry ghetto dwellers, many armed with clubs while others carry long household knives.

Horrified at finding themselves outnumbered, Gaius and Quintas unsheathe their swords and hold them up in defense, crying out while backing away with their weapons drawn, "Stay back! This is Caesar's business!" Their retreat is slow at first and then they turn and run, dodging a barrage of rocks with one good-sized stone smacking Gaius squarely in the back.

Having rid the ghetto of unwanted guests, a friend wraps his arms around Hillel's shoulders and cheers him, "Well done Hillel! You stood your ground. They must have been mad to enter our neighborhood with only two."

"Mad or desperate," remarks another neighbor. "You had better warn Judas and Jesus they are being sought."

The smoldering anger that began at the communal burial caves a few nights ago finally boiled over as many feared it would. In the city center, hundreds of townsfolk, angry over empty food stalls and costly goods fill the streets in a tense, uneasy protest. A radical preacher stands on a raised platform of broken stones and bricks and encourages the crowd to have their voices heard and their complaints addressed.

"We know suffering!" he shouts. "We suffered for a thousand years as slaves for the pharaohs, but it is worse under Herod and the Roman infidels! We can endure much without complaint, but with these invaders, there is no limit to their greed. Where is the food we harvest? Who steals our resources while we go without?"

"We starve while the Gentiles feast?" cries another.

The crowd cheers them on. "Death to the Invader! Death to the infidel! Death to Herod!"

At the Roman barracks, soldiers have come to life. Sensing the city about to riot, they secure their leather helmets onto their heads and strap on swords. As they exit, the men grab wooden batons and smack them loudly against their shields. The thundering sound of hundreds of clubs hitting shields intensifies the men's excitement along with commands from the officers intensify their resolve to quell the riot and arrest those responsible for it.

They mass on the parade ground and stand at attention in tight formation, waiting impatiently for the gate to open. When the command is given, they march through the open gate to the streets in an orderly manner. The ferocity of the group of seasoned fighters is accentuated by batons hitting their shields with every other step.

As they near the area of protest they quicken their pace and soon are nearly running at full speed through the streets. Nothing stands in their way to block their progress—carts are knocked aside, innocent onlookers are shoved out of their path or thrown up against buildings. Those who should have scrambled to safety earlier are knocked to the ground, trampled, or kicked aside.

A large group of ghetto dwellers lie in wait for the soldiers with an arsenal of stones, bricks, and rubble stacked in many large piles. When the soldiers enter the square they are met with hundreds of stone projectiles. Most bounce harmlessly off shields, but many find their mark and drop those unlucky soldiers to the ground. A Centurion on a horse watches in anger to see so many of his men toppled. He grits his teeth as progress comes to a halt and screams at his troops. "Attack! Attack now! Spare no one!"

The soldiers push on against a constant rain of flying stones. The Centurion is struck in the head by a large rock and falls to the ground unconscious. Infuriated, his troops press on, unconcerned for their safety. They mass close together to form a protective roof over their heads with their shields waiting for the rebels' stockpile of stones to become depleted. When the barrage lessens, the soldiers take the opportunity to surge forward.

The soldiers charge over the wall of debris and begin to strike down the fleeing protesters as they chase them through the streets, alleys, and over stone walls. Not all are a part of the chase as many duck into a door that conveniently opens for them.

The rout of the protesters creates a wall of fleeing bodies, forcing Judas and I to seek shelter by pressing ourselves into the deep recesses of a shop. We watch the soldiers race past, ignoring us as they are focused on the many targets directly before them. I hear the horrid crack of a baton striking a man's skull, soon followed by the bloodied man tumbling into our doorway and almost knocking me over. I pull him into the dark with us and out of sight of the soldiers.

The riot travels away from us as a violent caravan of beatings, screaming, and cursing, and I peer out the doorway and spot a nearby dark alley. I lift the injured man and race to the alley and I lay him on the ground. I tear a strip of cloth to wrap his head which should stop the bleeding.

As I am about to ask Judas what our next move should be, a second wave of soldiers appears. These are stragglers, slow-footed but large men who fell behind until sucking in a second wind. This group begins attacking the unfortunates who thought it safe to step out of their homes. A soldier trots past us to beat an already injured man. Another poor soul who is lying on his back and barely conscious, pleads for mercy as a soldier begins beating his legs with a baton.

Enraged, Judas races across the street and attacks the soldier. He bashes him in the back of the skull with his fist, then grabs the soldier's club and hits him on the torso at least three or four times. To keep Judas from killing the soldier, I leave the safety of the alley and pull him off the man. As I run back to the alley, another soldier who is beating a helpless man sees me, drops his victim and charges toward me with his club raised.

It is not the fight I fear—I fought plenty growing up in Joseph's shop or aboard ship with boys my age. That was a part of growing up, and I was good with my fists. But childhood scuffles do not prepare one to battle a grizzled soldier armed with a weapon. With no time to react, I duck down in a defensive position in anticipation of the blow I am about to receive when suddenly, Judas appears and strikes the soldier, knocking him to the ground at my feet. The soldier gaped at me in shock, puzzled at how he ended up on his back with me standing over him. Dulled by the blow, he still attempts to rise before Judas crushes his face with more than one powerful blow, and before he strikes again, I pull him off the unconscious soldier.

"That is enough! Let us go!" I yell.

As we dragged the soldier toward a street away from the injured protester we left in the alley, I heard more soldiers yell, "Down that street! Two of them!"

We drop the soldier and begin racing through the streets and leaping over walls, and scramble through gardens.

"We're almost free!" I say as I stop at a familiar building— one I helped build a foundation for under a merchant's shop. I push Judas through an opening at the base of the building and crawl in behind him.

"I think we've lost them," I gasp as I try not to make too much noise with my heavy breathing.

After a moment, I take a cautious peek through the small opening and it appears we have outdistanced the soldiers, losing them in the maze of streets and alleys of the old city. I turn back to find Judas sitting against the wall with darkness on his face, staring off into the blackness of the cellar.

"Are you feeling ill?" I ask.

"Ill, yes, that is what I feel. This occupation will never end. Leave me here, it no longer matters," complains Judas.

"Do not be so dramatic," I say. "There are better ways to die than on a Roman cross. Plus, I will need help with the poor fellows injured by the soldiers. Our night's work has just begun."

Judas shakes his head in disgust. "Stay close to me, then. I pledged to your father I would always keep an eye on you, so, if I have anything to say about it you will not die tonight"

We wait until we are certain the soldiers have left the streets and returned to their barracks and the streets are safe. We cautiously make our way through the city and it is eerily quiet except for a few smoldering bonfires. For many hours, I tended to the wounded, but despite the viciousness of the attack, most of the injuries were minor. The local townspeople leave the safety of their homes to sweep away the rocks and rubble left by the riot and greet us as we pass. In the distance, we hear a single cry of, "Death to the infidel!"

We locate our injured man sitting against the wall still dazed by the crack to his head. Judas runs to the end of the alley to ensure the route is clear.

"Can you walk?" I ask him. The man nods "yes," and I help him to his feet. Then, without warning, a blow strikes me, followed by the sound of a boulder smashing to the ground, and I am sent into darkness.

All is black until I am awoken by the face of a white angel with large, dark eyes and a long face licking my hair.

"Am I dead?" I ask myself.

I hear a distant voice ask, "Is he going to live?"

I fall into blackness again.

When I return to the light, I find I am in the home of Judas, lying on his cot with a cool towel wrapped about my head. I look across the room to the slightly blurred image of a woman sitting at a small table watching me.

"You have been out for some time," she says. "Quite a knock on the skull, but it looks like you will live."

My vision clears and I recognize her as a woman who goes by the name of Salome; a prostitute who also works with a group of zealots, sharing her body with Roman officials and Centurions. As a spy, she finds it is much easier to loosen their lips following many cups of wine with more secrets to be learned in the bed.

"I saw an angel," I say.

Salome laughs, "It was a horse. He was worried for you."

"There was a horse in the house?"

Salome laughs and says, "Judas returned to help the injured and found the poor thing stranded in a strange neighborhood. His master must have fallen during the battle, and without the call of the whip, the poor fellow decided it was a good time to desert his post."

Judas enters the dimly lit room with a great smile and an armful of towels and a jug of water. "It is good to see you awake my friend, how are we feeling?"

"Terrible," I reply. "Bless you for coming to my rescue. I hear you have a new Roman friend."

"It is reassuring to see you have not lost your good humor. What you say is true, but he will not be a Roman for long. I have hidden him in a barn and soon he will fetch a good price from the Oriental traders. He will have a much happier life as a Persian."

"I am surprised he let you take him."

"It appears he lost his love of battle after sustaining a serious wound to his hind leg. Maybe you could help him by using some of your magic tonics on it."

I feel the bump on my skull and thankfully it is a small one.

There is an area of coagulated blood on my hair and I guess that I hit the ground head first when I was attacked from behind.

I ask Judas, "Could I stay here for a bit, at least until my mind clears and my head stops pounding?"

"You know you may stay here as long as it takes," he replies. "If you can help the horse, I am eternally in your debt."

I return to sleep until I am startled awake by a dark silhouette touching my face. Instinctively, I grab the arm and throw the figure onto the bed, pinning him tightly under my weight. I raise my fist to strike him until I hear a woman's cry, and I immediately loosen my grip on what I now recognize as the slender arm of a woman. I begin to rise but she reaches up and pulls me to her.

"Jesus," she says.

It is the voice of Mary, but how is she here? Am I still in the dream? But she hugs me tightly and I feel the warmth of her skin and the shape of her narrow hips. This causes me great anxiety, and I feel...well, I am not certain what it is I feel, but she needs to release me.

Mary cries, "I was afraid you had been arrested. Judas told Yaron you were here, and...they said you were seriously hurt."

When Mary cries softly into my chest I push her away, then move to the edge of the bed and sit with my back to her. Again she reaches around my waist and holds me tight. I do not know what to do except hold her and stroke her hair until she calms.

"You should not be here," I finally say. "How did you avoid the soldiers?"

"Yaron showed me the way. He knows all the hidden paths. I heard so many were beaten and I knew you would not let those suffer if you could help them, and I needed to know you were safe."

It is dark but I can clearly see a stream of tears glistening on her cheeks and brush them aside. "There were many injured. I lost count of how many broken heads and battered faces I cared for until receiving the blow."

I feel the softness of her hair in my hands and the fragrance of roses on her skin. This certainly must be the moment when I tell her what I have wanted to say since we first met, which is what I do. "Mary, not a moment has passed without you in my thoughts."

"As it is with me," she says and holds me tighter.

I tell her of the night's rioting; attending to the wounded, Judas attacking the soldiers, and the two of us returning to retrieve the injured man before being struck.

She kisses my hands and it fills me with emotions I have never before felt. And almost stupidly think of what might become of us. In a thousand years, who will know the story of a young man and woman who found themselves falling in love during such troubling times as we now live in?

Mary reaches up and kisses me on the lips and I am struck by a thunderbolt. I pull away because it is not our custom to kiss on the lips, although I know of many cultures that do. She watches me with interest as I wrestle with my thoughts, waiting patiently, then ever so slowly our lips move closer until they meet and we hold our kiss. It is very pleasing and I realize that one could never feel true love unless they were willing to give body and soul to their partner.

I notice Mary's eyes are closed as if sight interferes with the kiss, so I close mine too. It is true, that the sensation is enhanced. We hold our embrace until the sound of Judas rattling around outside breaks the spell and ends this moment of paradise—short-lived but powerful enough to last a lifetime. How quickly our friendship has grown from playful flirting to a desire to spend my life her.

Judas knocks loudly and waits a moment before opening the door. The amused look on his face tells us he knows that love is in fresh bloom and fills the atmosphere. He walks to his table, grabs a jug of wine and drinks deeply, then tells us in great detail about the mood of the city.

"The Roman bastards are out in force pushing people around, looking for certain individuals who kicked their asses last night."

"That would include you," I say.

"You are correct," replies Judas. "They search for two men who go by the names of Judas and Jesus. Why we have been singled out is puzzling to me, except that two Roman thugs accosted Hillel and Eban looking for us. It appears our days in this miserable city are numbered."

"Who would have given them our names, and why?" I ask.

"I have my suspicions, and they lead straight to that drunkard we shoved. It makes no difference; we must make plans to flee."

"You may count on me to help with any expenses. I will give you whatever you need. You have your pay from work, also."

"Not to worry, my friend. When I sell that horse, I will have plenty of Persian gold. But you forget, they are looking for two men, so you need to devise a plan, too."

Mary tightens her hold on my hands and says, "Let me help. The soldiers on the road know me by sight and no longer inspect my cart. Judas could hide amongst the goods. Who would suspect a young man and woman escaping the violence?"

"Mary, you are under Joseph's care. You cannot run into the wilderness. He would never forgive me."

"Nonsense. I am a free woman and I will have you and Judas to accompany me."

I shake my head no. "Anywhere outside the city gates is

unsafe and unpredictable, and we are no kind of protection. The soldiers are agitated after being attacked. They might kill us for no other reason than they are deranged."

"I am not afraid," she says defiantly. "The road from Magdala was a much more dangerous journey and did I not avoid the Roman soldiers tonight? "

"Better yet," interrupts Judas, "is to keep you both safe from harm. I will have no problem evading the soldiers who rarely travel off their excellent paved roads. A little used dirt path will keep me sufficiently safe from those lazy bastards."

"Let me talk to Joseph," I say. "Maybe we can sneak you onto one of his ships."

"You can't endanger your uncle." Judas sits back on his stool and grins at us. "What has gotten into you two? Love has made you both completely mad. Listen, I am capable of escaping on my own, but if you two are going to be carrying on as you are, I suggest you both receive permission to do so."

I awake this morning still suffering with a lingering pain in my head but I am joyful and content. My thoughts are only of Mary, and how we talked late into the night—our first adventure and how brave she was as we made it safely through the back streets and hidden passageways. The bright moon guided us to Joseph's villa, where, at his gate, we embraced and kissed once more. It is possible we held each other for a long time, and as Judas mentioned, if we carry on like this we must have approval from those we respect. That is always my goal.

Entering the kitchen Father built for his growing family, I am always impressed at his building skills. Few homes in this land feature a built-in eating nook or a cool storage closet all in the same room. I am certain had he seen Uncle Joseph's sink, he would have installed one in this home.

I find Mother sitting by an open window rubbing the nose of a friendly young goat with its head poking through the opening. Mother has placed a spread of bread, fruit, olives, and even some boiled eggs on the table and I sit down and reach for a loaf of coarse bread. I glance at Mother and she looks especially radiant on this day. The morning sun seems to be bathing her in a bright, heavenly glow to my eyes.

"Mother, does the world know of your beauty?" I ask playfully. "It is a shame the goat is your only admirer."

"Please do not tease," she says quietly.

I realize too late that she is in no mood for any silliness. I bury my face in the food and think, *if she only knew what happiness I am feeling, she might enjoy the teasing.* Instead, she stands abruptly and moves about the kitchen putting away crockery, banging iron pots around, and wiping clean her counter.

I look up and ask her, "What, I cannot tell my mother she is beautiful?"

She turns to me with a tight smile and says. "Thank you."

As I continue shoving food into my mouth, the truth of her ill humor is revealed as she begins asking me too many questions, "Why have you slept so late? Were you involved in the rioting? You leave no word of your whereabouts and only come home to change your clothes and eat. I have no idea what you are up to. And your friends, why, they all look like criminals!"

"Most of them are," I laugh. "But those criminals, as you call them, put food on the table working for us."

Mother returns to her seat at the window and I watch her

out of the corner of my eye while attacking the food like the starved beggar that I am. Her disapproving look has me waiting for what will certainly be more criticism of my life.

I do not have to wait very long. "I beg you, please turn away from this rebellion and return to the temple," she pleads. "I miss your sermons, and your words were so beautiful."

Not this morning, I moan to myself. "Those were not my words," I replied between gulps of bread and water. "I parroted the words of other men's knowledge and used them as my own. I was nothing more than a boastful, self-centered child."

"You were a beautiful, kind boy. Do not demean yourself."

"Mother, I have no wisdom to share. And who in this town has not heard me a hundred times?"

"You are young and impatient, I understand, but our people need to know what God has promised!"

"What should I preach now that the church has allied itself with the invaders? No one believes in them any longer."

"Do not blaspheme!"

"It is not I who blaspheme, it is the priests who demand payment for prayer. It is ludicrous! It would be better if we simply started over with a new God—one who doesn't require endless demand for our coins."

Mother gasps in shock and I wish I could retract that last sentiment. My mother has so much faith in God, it is not right that we battle.

"I am sorry, Mother, I do not mean to cast doubt on the faith. But on this earth, the poor need food and shelter. The slums grow larger every day while the church grows fat and rich. You see that I am working to help our people. Why do you demand that should I be lecturing them also?"

162

I once believed that the Golden Temple was God's house. As I traveled to other lands I learned that everything is God's house: the air and water, trees, birds, the soil—everything we know and feel, is God. Why build a golden temple when nothing compares to the genius of a tree or the vast universe that stares down upon us? The money changers and the priests have their gold, but their money will not save them once the Romans grow tired of our never-ending revolts and wipe us and our religion off the face of the earth.

Mother leans against the sill and rests her head in her hand. "I had always hoped that our lives might have been different."

Her voice drifts off and she returns to petting the goat.

After everything that has happened to our family because she dreamed of the angel and those men from Persia who nearly got us all killed, how can she still cling to such false hope?

"Who has come to my aid and given me advice in this mission of mine you've talked about my entire life?" I ask.

"Let us not argue anymore," she says. "It is obvious it will not be your mother's pleadings that change your heart."

Mother is right. There is only one person in my life who now softens my pain—a different kind of love than that of a parent. This love fills the soul greater than any other, and I know the news I am about to tell her will brighten her day.

"I do have something to tell you—some very good news."

I wait until I am certain I have her full attention before I say, "I am hoping Mary will accept my proposal to wed."

I hold my breath awaiting Mother's response. The room grows silent, and now I am not certain how Mother is reacting to this announcement. I see her lips tighten, staring at me, unblinking.

"Mary, the girl from Magdala? The girl living in Joseph's home? When did this happen...how did you meet?"

"We became friends while I was working at the villa. Mother, she is the one I want to spend my life with. I desire your approval more than you can ever know. What is your answer?"

And there it is. For the first time since Joseph was killed, my mother's beautiful dark eyes light up and she smiles. She comes to my side and wraps her arms around me.

"If this is what you wish for, you have my blessing. Joseph has told me many good things about this girl, and I think she will be a fine partner for you. Let us draw up the contract and present it to your uncle."

I am delighted to feel her love again. She calms at our touch and her tenderness flows to me like a river. Who would not want a mother pleased with their son's choice of a wife?

I left the church because of the children killed in Bethlehem. So, where do I find the holy spark and wisdom, and how could I possibly counsel others when there is so much turmoil within me? I notice Mother's hands and how they have aged, and there is a slight tremble to them. If I had more knowledge, I would know how to heal the diseases inside the body, such as leprosy and blindness that cripple and kill us. Maybe my destiny is to become a healer. What other reason is there to explain why I possess this gift?

As if reading my mind, Mother takes my hands and brings them to her cheek. "Don't let the past control your life, son. It is you who they sacrificed everything for."

How does one erase the past?

"With a wife by your side, maybe you would gain what you lost since you abandoned your mission. Surely you see that more than ever our people need to know God's plan. If you continue to ignore what was foretold, then Herod has won and you will have given victory to the enemies of God."

My short-lived happiness has quickly dissolved into her vision for me, and we find ourselves discussing my destiny once again. I am in love with Mary and that's all I care about.

I am tired, my head still hurts, and I need Mother to end her sermon or my suffering will never cease. She also needs to know that I am a wanted man, so I blurt out, "Judas beat two soldiers and stole a Centurion's horse during the riots. For some reason, they have learned of our names and they are looking for us."

Mother blinks in disbelief. "Oh son, this is exactly what I was afraid of. And how do you expect to ask this girl to marry when you are now considered an enemy?"

"I was hoping we might flee by hiding in one of Uncle's ships. We could begin a new life elsewhere."

Mother gasps and brings her hands to her mouth while shaking her head repeatedly and saying, "He would be ruined if any insurgent is discovered aboard any of his ships. What are you thinking?"

"I thought we might sail up the coast to meet one of his ships safely away from the Romans." Last night I thought it to be a very good plan. However, in the light of day, it appears to have been a terrible idea.

Mother folds her hands in her apron and thinks for a moment before saying, "You cannot involve Joseph. He is an important member of the community and his wealth provides food and work for many. Judas is more than capable enough to survive on his own. It is what he has done since we first took him in. If you insist on going through with this marriage and dragging that poor girl with you into hiding, you must have protection and allies to give you a safe harbor."

"What do you suggest then?"

Mother grows quiet for a moment, and I am almost certain what is coming next. "You are a builder," she says. "What is the most important element of any structure, no matter how great or small?"

"A good foundation," I reply.

"There, that is your answer. What you desire most is to know the truth about your birth—that is your foundation. When you discover the truth, you will be able to live with yourself and follow your destiny, whatever that may be."

"And where will I find this truth?" I ask.

"There are several villages far from the reach of Rome's tentacles. You would be safe and protected in those towns as most of them have no love for the Romans or Herod."

"Do you have a particular village in mind?"

"As I said, there are many I could think of, but only one knows of you and would welcome you. You have always wanted to learn about those who were sacrificed so that you might live—it is the source of your pain. Why not go to them?"

Mother has never strayed from a path she believes was shown to her nineteen years ago. Whether she is right or not, Bethlehem would be a good place to hide until the Romans grow tired of looking for me. It is not as if I am the only man named Jesus in this land.

"Who would I go to? The children are dead."

The brightness in my mother's eyes makes me smile. They lighten up at the prospect of me in Bethlehem. She has come alive, the one who has suffered so much, more than I, but her faith has never failed.

"You were not the only one chosen by our Father," she says. "The people of Bethlehem were also chosen because of their strong faith in the Lord."

It is strange to think that others gambled everything hoping for a miracle that I would deliver. I wonder how they fared after such a tragedy, and will Bethlehem be the place where I will finally learn the truth? Whether true or not, how could I ever repay those who sacrificed so much?

Mother perceives a crack in my shield—a small one, but an opening, and nothing else needs to be said between us. I rise from the table and hug her, which she gratefully and warmly returns for the first time in many months.

"I wonder, will I be welcomed in Bethlehem? Some may still resent what happened to them because of us."

"I pray that is not what you will find. Your father and I did not abandon them to Herod's soldiers. We begged them to take their children and flee with us, but they knew what God was asking of them and refused to leave."

How many years has that horrific event affected me, unable to move forward because of this entity we praise and worship? A cruel master, who according to the prophets, has promised a young woman, my mother, a great gift to the world: His Son, but for what purpose? The answer has never come to me, even though I was protected from the knife because of the miracle of Joseph's dream. Am I to end up as the latest in a long line of saviors who failed to open the gates of the Kingdom for the people of Israel? It was the sea that saved me and showed me more of the world than our dusty little corner of the Empire ever could have. The world is filled with a thousand different tribes and races who worship thousands of Gods—every one powerful, glorious, and cruel.

Those who study the gifts of this earth, who heal and save lives, such as my teacher, the physician, or those who use their knowledge of the stars, the wind, and the sea, who sail to lands previously unknown—those are the men I have chosen to follow.

My thoughts fill my head and I hear mother speaking to me from a great distance. "Wise men still live in Bethlehem, son. Go there. Talk to them and discover the truth."

I rise from the table and roughly pat the goat on the head as I leave the kitchen. I seek a moment of peace to clear my head in a small wood-slatted shed filled with hens, rabbits, and pigeons. I come here often to think, beginning after Joseph was killed. I spent many days wondering why God swept my father away for no apparent reason, especially after Bethlehem. I would stare at my tears as they fell to the dry earth, then watch the dirt absorb every drop and leave no trace of my sad contribution. Like our lives, most leave no evidence of our existence. My outcome, and whatever happens to me are of little importance—truth is what matters.

THE ROAD TO BETHLEHEM

In our culture, it is undesirable to marry a woman from a foreign clan lest she introduce false beliefs and practices. But had my father lived, he would happily have chosen Mary to be my wife, foreign beliefs or not. Our marriage is grounded in love, so the Shadkhan, the matchmaker who brokers the contract between the joining of two families was not necessary in our case.

Mary and I are wed after the ritual of Tevilah, which is the immersion of the entire body in water for the purpose of removing ritual impurity. In attendance is Mother, my brothers James, Joses, Judas, Simon, Joseph's family, and Mary's companion, Sarah. My only regret on this, the finest of days, is the absence of Judas who has fled the city.

We stroll through the gardens and orchards until we reach the very highest point of the property looking out to the blue sea. A table is waiting for us there decorated with flowers and laden with wine, fruits, bread, and meat. My uncle, a man of few words and not known to express his emotions openly, has something to say about this marriage, so he begins by asking us to join hands and bow our heads. We stand quietly for a few moments listening to the sounds of nature—flying insects, crickets, and birds.

"The kingdom of heaven is a hidden treasure awaiting discovery," begins Joseph. "I only ask of this remarkable young couple is to pursue the sacred counsel of their souls, which urge them on to virtue. Let neither danger nor the encumbering world diminish their love for each other and life's purpose. May your steps bring you to bliss and crown your future with peace."

On our first day as man and wife, Mary and I are gifted privacy in an apartment near the pool to enjoy our new life together. For a moment the world's ills are vanquished as we spent the afternoon in the pool, lounging on comfortable couches, and making plans for the upcoming journey to Bethlehem.

When the sun dropped below the sea, we consummated our wedding as tradition dictates and one we eagerly looked forward to and enjoyed with immense pleasure. I was reminded of Judas' comment that with such a beauty lying beneath me, I should expect to have many children.

In the late evening, as we walked together through the olive grove overlooking the city, reality presented itself to us once again. A small building was set afire near the Roman barracks, followed shortly by the sounds of yelling, cursing, and of course, an army of barking dogs joining in.

We began our journey following two groups of Nabataean traders' caravan and after many security checkpoints, we made it past the last post located far into the countryside. As Mary predicted, none of the soldiers harassed us, and I discovered they even had a very protective inclination toward her. When she told them of our marriage, all congratulated us and waved us through, one checkpoint after another. Observing how my wife had enchanted these men made me very proud and reminded me of how fortunate I was to have her by my side.

We traveled a circuitous route, far away from our destination of Bethlehem to the oasis of En-Gedi, a thriving little estate located near the Dead Sea at the foot of a flat hill named, Tel Goren. The heavily fortified town acted as a vault for a portion of Mary's inheritance. Although I can provide for us, Mary demands she not be dependent on anyone, including me. It is also important to her that she has enough funds to continue her work caring for the poor.

There are inns and rooms available within the walls of the city, but we decided to make our encampment instead by the natural spring pools that form the En-Gedi oasis under endless rows of date palms, citrus orchards, and fields of produce irrigated by the water found in natural cisterns deep within the rocks of Tel Goren. We rest under the swaying palms under a small canopy I constructed, lying together on a blanket and lost in quiet meditation. I turn onto my stomach and watch the donkey for a spell as it lazily munches on a small pile of dry grass and appears to be as happy as I am.

Nearby, the Nabataean traders have set up a dozen colorful tents and talk non-stop while they busy themselves roasting meat on skewers over a large pit.

Mary scoots close, rests her head on my shoulders, and asks, "Tell me about the days before you sailed on your uncle's ships."

I stare off into a cloudless blue sky and take a deep breath. It is not a period in my life I am proud of. Before Mary, I had never spoken to anyone but Judas about my break with the family. I felt I had a legitimate right to have been angry with the world, right or not, it was how I felt at the time.

"I entered my thirteenth year in a constant state of war with my parents and anyone else who crossed me. I was fighting at work, with my younger siblings who were always underfoot and constantly disturbing my studies. I battled everyone."

"What was it that made you so difficult?"

"Most children at this age can become troublesome, do you not think?"

Mary ponders this for a few moments. "Not honoring your parents is sinful, but this mostly seems to be a problem in families with wealth. The poor do not have that luxury."

"I do not disagree. The truth is, it was when I discovered the story of Bethlehem and the killing of the children."

I feel Mary squeeze my hand tighter. "I am so sorry," she says, which is pretty much all that can be said about that event.

"My parents decided that time away from the people who reminded me of my past might be a wise course of action. They felt by setting me out to sea I might return a better person. It turned out that they were right."

"They sent you away, on a ship? Destined to where?"

"My first voyage was a brief one to Egypt."

"Were you afraid? Had you ever been on the sea?"

"No! Their suggestion filled my mind with fantasy, imagining strange new lands, and battling monsters of the deep. The reality was that there was much less fantasy and mostly hard work. But I fell in love with the sea and the older sailors who told us young boys adventurous stories. They were a treat to listen to and they talked incessantly, which relieved the monotony of work. One of the games they constantly played, even while working, was who could tell the biggest lie. Whoever told the best story, got an extra pull on the jug of wine."

"Did you ever win an extra portion of wine?" teases Mary.

"The boys were not allowed to participate and we would not have stood a chance of winning anyway. Not long after setting sail, the yeoman discovered my expertise with the saw and hammer and took me on as his apprentice carpenter. Most boys are assigned to the galley or become a Captain's Boy, so it was a very proud moment for me to know that my skills were appreciated thanks to my father and years of training.

On my second voyage, we sailed to Britannia to pick up tin and lead for Roman plumbing, the same kind of material used in that sink Judas and I were installing when I first saw you." I glance at Mary to make certain she's still interested in my story.

She is gazing at me with a sly grin. "How interesting! The same material you transported from Britannia was forged in fire and made into a sink then shipped to Joppa where you and Judas installed it in your uncle's home."

"Where it would drive us mad," I laugh.

"But your cursing would be the reason we met and fell in love," chides Mary.

"This tale might win me a pull on the jug." I laugh and lean down and kiss her. "But, it is true, and we are in love, so I'll continue if you're still amused."

"So far," she replies with a warm smile.

"As we neared the coast of Britannia, the captain assigned me the task of assisting the ship's physician in gathering medicinal herbs and material from a village a short distance from the harbor. We filled the wagon with goods brought for barter and drove from the harbor through dense a green forest.

"Is Britannia as beautiful as I imagine?"

"Maybe even more so. I spent the drive gaping in wonder at the many large trees, plants, and flowers, and all on a smooth stone road built by the Romans two hundred years earlier."

"They are a strange people," says Mary. "Despite their

penchant for cruelty, they are industrious. How far out to sea did you travel, and what lies beyond Britannia and the watery dessert?"

"Throughout the journey, we never saw land except for a few islands off the coastline of Gaul. Beyond the narrow opening of the Pillars of Hercules, and once free from the confines of Mare Internum, the captain directed his course to Britannia by the stars. As far as I could see, there was no end to the great river of Oceanus, which I have been told is immense and ends only when it runs into the cosmos and the heavens."

"Is that where heaven lies?" asks Mary.

"So it is said. I believe it would take many lifetimes to reach such a place. From Joppa to Britannia alone, a distance that takes over one hundred days, we never left what is considered the Roman Empire, and the Empire covers only a small portion of the earth."

I feel I am boring my dear wife, but she eagerly waits for me to continue. "Tell me about Britannia," she asks, "what was it like? What did the people look like?"

"Unlike you and I, they are very light-skinned, even more so than the Romans. But they do possess a certain physical beauty once you become used to it. Upon seeing them for the first time, Egyptian sailors called them ghosts because of their thin, small noses. But the men are fierce warriors and decorated in skin tattoos, even on their faces. The women are also fierce warriors. Mary, you will like this as they are equal partners in everything, from marriage, to war, and commerce."

"So, it is not an illness I have as some have complained," says Mary. "There were some who accused me of possession if you can believe that. Most were members of my own family as they plotted to rob me of my inheritance."

"They are fools."

"Thank you, my love," she says and kisses me. "Now husband, tell me more."

"As you wish. The road from the harbor to the village was a beehive of activity, filled with carts carrying goods to and from the harbor. All the while, the physician described the many plants along the way, continually pointing out those that the Britons and others used for medicine and healing. He said the forest was a bountiful market for any healer who knew his business, and that the earth provided everything we needed to sustain life. All that was required was to look to nature for answers. He believed nature is where God lies.

"The priests might disagree with your philosophy," I said.

"'What is just and what is unjust?' he replied. 'That is a study in humanity. God is in all things—look around. Unlike man, there is order and harmony in nature. That perfection is God.'"

I continued to press him—the boastful young scholar who had spent his youth attending synagogue. I consider myself very knowledgeable about the origins of life. "The priests tell a different story," I argued, "and they are very learned men."

The physician shrugged and shook his head. "What man has learned is but a handful of dirt. What is left unlearned is the earth itself."

"What an interesting man," says Mary. "How long did you stay with him?"

"I begged the ship's captain to let me study with the physician, and he agreed that I could as long as I did my other chores. I sailed with the physician for more than four years."

"That explains your abilities as a healer."

"The physician told me there was so much that has been given to us that a lifetime of learning would not be enough to know more than a small portion of it."

"Tell me more about the people," asks Mary.

"Let me think. Yes! I did experience a wild-looking young woman who stalked me like prey. She was fascinated by my dark skin and could not stop touching me. The physician pulled me aside and told me to avoid her as she was a sin-eater. In this part of the world, a piece of bread was placed on the chest of the recently departed, and the sin-eater was paid a silver coin to eat the bread and take on the sins of the deceased."

"How odd. Was she a priestess?"

"No. She was shunned until needed, an outcast who lived apart from the village in the forest."

Mary grows silent as she imagines this girl's life. "What a terrible burden. Why would she take it on? When she dies, does she take the sins with her, or does a new sin-eater take on her sins so that the predecessor may enter heaven with a pure soul? Why is she shunned if they call on her to take away other's sins? Is it because she takes money for her service?"

She fires many questions at me rapidly, forcing me to laugh out loud.

"I am serious, Jesus. Do not mock me."

"I would never. But I do not think it is much different than paying the money changers at the Temple for the sacrifice. Maybe it is a calling or a curse handed down from previous generations of family members. I do not know."

"We release a goat during Yom Kipper to absolve us of our sins," exclaims Mary. "Do you not find it interesting that there are so many overlapping traditions in other religions?"

"Yes, it is why Mother and I battled frequently. Most religious texts contain stories that appear across different faiths—the same stories repeat themselves again and again throughout history."

"You do love your mother, do you not? She is such a kind and pious woman, and very beautiful too. It is why you are so handsome."

"I do love my mother, and I honor the tradition of respecting one's elders and parents. And I understand her burden, maybe of her own making, but she has never wavered in her faith, which is impressive. She and Father sacrificed much because of her vision, and it was that vision that allowed me to study with the greatest teachers. Unfortunately, the more I learned, the more I discovered that many of the texts written by the scribes were fabricated. I know there was good reason for this deception—rules, and morals needed to be established to govern a people unaccustomed to freedom. But, that does not mean they came directly from God."

When I roll onto my back, Mary lays her head on my chest and we enjoy the sound of the desert breeze rustling through the palm leaves.

Moments later, Mary lifts her head and asks, "Tell me more about your travels."

"If that is your desire. You might find this interesting. After leaving the village of the sin-eater, we traveled to another village nearby where the physician filled his barrels from a well of what he said was healing water."

"Like the heated water in the Roman baths?"

"No, this water was more of a tonic. The physician told me to take notice of the local people, and when I did, I saw that their skin was without flaw. I saw no evidence of leprosy or lesions of any sort. This water contained a substance that cured all sorts of maladies. Drinking it helped with stomach issues, and applying it to burned skin helped in healing without scars. Remember the vial

I gave to the child for his eye? It was water from this same village, and we paid a healthy price for the water, too."

"They must have become very rich selling water to traders and physicians," remarks Mary.

"If their prosperous-looking town was any indication of it, yes, they were very wealthy. Many years earlier, the Romans had built an elaborate stone temple there, giving that holy water the importance it deserved.

"Did those people have a water god?" asks Mary.

"They have many gods," I reply. "Coventina was popular in Aquae Sulis, the name of this town. She was the Goddess of healing springs. Mostly though, the Britons worshiped the sun, the god that gives life to the earth."

"It sounds as if your physician agreed with that concept," teases Mary. "Did you see any places of worship?"

"I am certain they had some, but I never saw any. They had totems though. The entrance to nearly every village was a carved wooden post with a hideous face, large bulging eyes, and a fierce mouth with sharpened bones for teeth. Its crown was covered with human hair and colored beads—a truly frightening creation."

"Would that be to protect the village from evil spirits?"

"Yes, she was called Frea. She protected the village, from evil spirits such as the Wolfman, and the Moor stalkers—living creatures that could snatch you off the road and carry you into the dark woods."

"Dear me," says Mary. "That land sounds horrible and magical...moor stalkers?"

"As I said, these were legends. You were more likely to be robbed by an outlaw dressed as a wolf than a demonic spirit."

"As terrible as those gods seem," says Mary, "it is interesting that they worship gods who are women."

"Yes, the most horrible women imaginable," I laugh.

I turn onto my side and watch my wife as she gazes up at the palm leaves lost in thought, transfixed by their eternal dance with the wind, and then she slowly closes her eyes and falls asleep. The wind plays with wisps of her hair and the shadows of the palm leaves move in slow motion across her face and I am reminded of an ancient Egyptian poem:

The breath of thy nostrils alone
Is that which makes my heart live
I found thee! Amen grant unto me,
Eternally and forever!

I lean down and kiss her softly on the lips. Mary, my wife, a woman to whom many would give all they own just to touch her hand. I lie on my back and fall asleep, too.

An uneasiness wakes me. An approaching unseen presence has me reaching for my knife and walking to the edge of the oasis for a look. I spot the silhouette of a man appearing to be walking on water, disappearing, then reappearing in the ghostly reflections of a mirage. As the man draws close he begins racing across the shimmering false lake at a fast pace. With each step, he grows larger, kicking up a cloud of dust as he runs, and is almost upon us before I recognize him to be my friend, Judas.

Without acknowledging my presence, Judas charges past and jumps into the water head first. He dives deep before surfacing and splashing about the pool. After a final dive, he comes to the surface and erupts with laughter.

The traders camping nearby verbally curse us, in a language I do not understand, and I offer them an embarrassed smile and apologize for my friend's behavior in a language they do not understand. They are offended but are also far from home and do not seek any trouble, so they turn away and return to their own business. I surmise they are upset, talking with animated hand gestures with an occasional hostile glance toward Judas in the pool. In an arid land like this, I understand why they are distressed—this water is not for bathing, but for drinking only.

"The journey was an endless one," laughs Judas, still up to his neck in the pool. "Anticipating the cool taste of water turned hours into days! And now, an even greater surprise—a joyful reunion with the two of you!"

"Do you think you were followed?" I ask.

"Vultures were dogging me the entire way, waiting for me to drop. I can assure you, any search for Judas will fail."

Mary also senses the uncomfortable hostility from the Arab traders. She digs through our bags and encourages Judas to leave the pool by standing at the water's edge and motioning him out of the pool with a clean cloth. He obediently climbs out and rips off his wet, filthy clothing, then tosses them to the ground with a scowl on his face as if they were diseased.

A few of the Arab traders whistle at him and his nakedness, which Judas enjoys to no end. Thank goodness his humor has lessened the tension. I search for dry clothing from my bags while Mary retrieves fruit and bread, and places them on the blanket.

"Once I refresh myself with your offering of sustenance, I'll beg those merchants' forgiveness for offending them," laughs Judas. "My body took over upon the sight of water and it was either full immersion or watch my skin erupt into flames. The way was far more grueling than I anticipated."

We take full advantage of this respite to pass a loaf of bread and share a jug of wine. Judas asked me if we had any trouble getting through the barricades.

"There were many, but nearly everyone congratulated Mary on her marriage to, such a fine young man."

"Good grief," laughs Judas, "Zealots should be led by women if it is so easy to deceive the soldiers. Well, you are a more fortunate man than I, having almost crawled here on my hands and knees so as not to be spotted. I nearly froze to death at night, and I might never recover from the rocks acting as a poor excuse for bedding."

Without warning, Judas throws his arms around me in a bear hug and easily wrestles me to the ground onto my back. "You're getting soft and slow my young friend. This marriage business has turned you into a weakling!"

Mary laughs, "I had no idea our marriage contract mentioned a large, violent child."

Judas looks at me with a sly grin. "Once you two have settled in, will I still be invited to sample Mary's excellent cooking?"

Judas forgets nothing and neither do I. "Do you still promise to watch the children while we escape to our secret hillside cave?"

"Absolutely! The finest breads, yes? As you promised?"

"None better in this land."

Puzzled by this secret dialogue, Mary scrutinizes Judas, then back to me quizzically. "What are you two on about?" she asks.

We shrug our shoulders and laugh like two schoolboys, then raise a toast to the future.

Mary joins us and chimes in, "Whatever it is you two have planned, I am going to keep Judas to that promise I just heard him make to watch over our many children."

Evening comes and we patiently await the stew Mary has been cooking over the fire all afternoon. The spicy, pungent scent wafts through the encampment and even the Arab merchants look over and nod their heads in approval.

Judas announces he has a gift for Mary and pulls a small leather pouch from his tunic. He kneels before her and hands her the small gift. "I know it's not our custom to bestow gifts for the marriage, but it should be for those you truly care about."

Mary excitedly unties the pouch and discovers a beaded, seed necklace with two gold crosses bound together in a decorative filigree of gold thread.

"Oh, Judas, it is beautiful!" exclaims Mary. "Put it on me!"

Mary lifts her hair for Judas as he places the necklace around her neck and secures it with a small gold lock.

"These two crosses represent the love you and Jesus share," he says almost in a whisper. "May you never part, no matter what may come your way."

Mary places a tender kiss on his cheek.

I am stunned as I have never heard Judas utter any words of endearment to anyone for anything.

"For a thousand years, the cross has been a sign of peace. It is also the Zealot's secret sign," continues Judas. "Now you are one of us."

"I shall never remove it! Thank you!" exclaims Mary.

"When did you find the time to have them made?" I ask.

"When I went over to the merchants to apologize. I noticed one of them was an artisan with some very fine ornamental works of art. So, I asked if he could make something for me."

"It is a wonderful gift, but you might need your purse."

Judas laughs. "I sold that Roman horse for a very good price. Oh yes, the Persians were very impressed with your healing skills, especially the use of honey to keep out the infection that saved the leg. I will find work if necessary, or we can work together as we have always done. There are plenty of jobs to be found in Jerusalem."

I awake that night from a dream-filled sleep of a ferocious battle taking place. Massive boulders were being fired from catapults and slamming into the stone walls of a fortress. Each strike erupted in my head with a powerful explosion and finally startled me awake. At first, I was afraid I had suffered a seizure and was relieved to discover myself unharmed. Still, I wonder what brought this on—a dream or the result of the injury to my head? To be able to look inside the body might seem macabre to some, but I know that many answers lie within, physically and spiritually. The cure for many of our ailments lies in waiting for discovery.

I search a night sky filled with stars and wonder what discoveries there are to be found. Those distant points of light allow us to navigate the seas, track time, and tell us the proper cycles for planting and harvesting. Are there others living on a star, watching us while we toil and war for the conquest of lands that are nothing more than specks of dust to them? I poke a stick at a few weak embers and think of the stars and the sea, and how vast they are. We have ventured far from land into the unknown water of Oceanus because we are a curious animal, but I wonder if we will ever discover the secret of the heavens. The remains of our campfire return to life with a snap and a crackle and I think how just a little prodding is all it takes to bring a fire back to life. It is the same with me...lessons to be learned surround me, even in a simple campfire.

Judas has wandered over to the encampment of the merchants and is dancing about the fire, probably boasting of his latest battle with the Romans. He ducks and swings, pantomiming his daring attack. Maybe only one or two of them speak Hebrew, but all share in the laughing as he tells his story.

I watch Mary sleep and I remain astounded that Mary is my wife. Maybe it is true love where heaven is found, and why did I not already know this? Mary knows, of this I am certain. Why else would a young woman leave the comforts of home to face almost certain hardships? She must have tremendous faith in our love and my ability to be a good husband, and I promise to prove to her that her choice was a good one. I wrap a blanket around my shoulders and turn my thoughts to the dark desert beyond—a noisy void filled with crickets and their rhythmical song—the pulse of life.

"Jesus, wake up, the camp is empty," says Mary.

Her hair awakes me to a beautiful vision—Mary's large green eyes surrounded by a halo of red hair.

"Are we married?" I ask.

She laughs. "Of course, we are my love. Have you already forgotten?"

"I was afraid it was a dream."

Mary leans in and kisses me. "Are you still dreaming?"

I might still be dreaming, life itself may be a dream. But if it is a dream, this moment is certainly a heavenly one.

"They left quietly," mumbles a sleepy Judas.

I laugh. "You were such a joy to watch, dancing around their campfire singing praises of your bravery."

"Nonsense!" cries Judas. "I only went over to tell them how much you liked their craftsmanship and to keep my eye on them. Artists and merchants are the worst sort of creatures. You are lucky I was on guard so they had no way to rob you, or cut your throats while you soundly slept."

"Judas! Those men were honest merchants," says Mary.

Judas eyes the empty campsite of the traders. "Trust no one

on the road," he warns. "Surprises abound around every corner and under every rock. There are no laws in the wilderness."

"Tell me, now that we have savored Mary's fine cooking and are gathered together in friendship, what plans are brewing?" asks Judas.

"We will be traveling to a small town not far from here and should be there by tomorrow," says Mary.

"Does this place have a name?"

"Bethlehem," I add.

The smile on Judas' face drops like a stone and he stares into the pool for a moment. He gapes at me, puzzled. "Bethlehem, the origin of your misery? Why not journey to the lands of the East? I hear many splendid cities are to be found there, and it is far from the Romans."

I reply solemnly, "I have to know the truth."

Judas beams a wide smile and pats me on the back, "If that is your desire, and this journey leads us to the golden shores of heaven, then so be it!"

TOUR OF DUTY

Our captain is a short, stocky, bull-dog of a man, who enters the room and stomps to a halt. He has a map in his hand and unfolds it with a snap before laying it out on the table. We continue to stand at attention while he ignores us and studies the map silently.

"At ease, men," he orders quietly before waving us to gather around the map. "We got a tense situation, " he growls and jabs the map with his finger. "Right here! A walled-in city overrun by a bunch of pissed-off insurgents. These turd-brains have managed to trap a group of French doctors working for the Red Cross, and the fuck-heads now realize they're trapped behind the walls. They're willing to release the French guys if we promise not to kick their asses and let 'em leave without incident. Our assignment is to bring those doctors back home, unharmed if at all possible."

The captain looks up from the map and glares at me. He's not the same CO I had on my first tour, but he probably read my file, or he might have heard some scuttlebutt from other officers. The military is a tight-knit family, and trust once lost, is difficult to regain. I'm surprised they called me back at all except that they need translators now that the locals are too afraid to work with us.

"Valdez, you're gonna be the Grand Marshall of this parade. When you get to the gates, you get on the loudspeaker and rattle off some of that Arab shit you know. You make sure these people know we're all about peace and love and don't want to see anyone

In what is considered livable conditions in the Marine Corps, I and a dozen other Marines find ourselves in a glorified tent with a noisy air conditioner working overtime to keep out the desert heat. We're cleaning our weapons and stuffing our packs with energy bars, clothing, and a dozen other non-military, personal items. Protection from incoming rockets and the weather is a fiberglass quonset-hut, built in two days by Navy Seabees whose motto is, "We build, we fight."

We joke it should be, "We build, they fight."

Home is a long narrow room with two rows of twin-size cots separated by rows of metal lockers. A table with built-in benches runs the entire length of the room, which in the past was used for folding clothes and writing letters until private contractors forbade us to do our own laundry. It pissed off our captain who is a serious Marine who thinks laundry duty is good for morale and promotes a gung-ho attitude necessary to survive. "What next?" he complained, "Paying civilians to clean our weapons? Bullshit bureaucrats!"

The laundry is a complete waste of time in this dusty part of the world anyway, and now the table is only used for writing letters to our girlfriends and wives back home. You'd be surprised how many relationships are sealed with an engagement ring just before shipping off to war.

At the moment I'm staring at a photo of Mimi and me embracing on the steps of our little house. The photo makes me sad as it was snapped the day before I got called back to Iraq. Absolute happiness is fleeting, but we have it in spades. The photo also reminds me that I owe Mimi everything I can do to make it home in one piece and ask her to marry me.

A gruff, deep voice yells out, "Atten-hut!" and everyone drops what they're doing and does as ordered.

get hurt. This is a rescue mission, but if any dumb shit decides to engage us, we're gonna fuckin' unload on 'em. Comprende?"

"Abeebi ma fi 'Zayrak b Zayete el shi wazeed li mazbout," I answer, which means: "My love, there's only you in my life, the one thing that shines bright."

The captain furrows his thick brow and directs a dark scowl at me before growling, "Whatever you just said, you insubordinate dick-head, someday I'm gonna get my own personal translator and find out the kind of shit you've been dishin' me. And when I do, I'm gonna kick your fuckin' ass!"

A simultaneous, "Ooh," erupts from the company.

Captain glares at us, one Marine at a time and you can hear a pin drop as he gives us his most frightening black look. Satisfied that he has thoroughly creeped everyone out, he cracks a wide evil grin and laughs his ass off. "You fucking pansies! Move out! And don't come back without those goddamn hostages!"

I kiss the photo of Mimi and place it carefully in the pocket over my heart. Then I close my eyes, place both hands over the photo and say quietly, "I love you too, Mimi."

The roads, barren hills, destroyed farms, and the few trees still standing are all covered in dust. The APC engine noise is no match for the sound of the Clash blasting through "Rock the Casbah," sounding contrived given our peaceful mission. The mood is one of nervous intensity, jive-talking and bullshit. Bullshit, because no one wants to be here. We've all done multiple tours and the violence hasn't stopped one bit. Beyond the windshield, the road stretches across empty rocky hills and mountains as far as the eye can see. I wonder why anyone would be fighting over this Middle Eastern dust bowl? Plus, it's at least one hundred degrees in the shade, if you can find any shade. I look in the side mirror and the view is even worse—clouds of dust obscure a dozen APCs following our lead. Thank god I'm leading this parade as the captain says, instead of eating dust.

Rosales, a young Tejano sitting shotgun, shouts, "Hey Valdez, what did you say to Captain America anyway? Did you let him know he has his head up his ass?"

Corporal Adams and Davis, the two Marines riding in the back in full battle rattle (at least fifty pounds of gear, including flak vests, Kevlar helmet, gas mask, and ammunition), laugh and join in. Adams, a veteran of at least three deployments and still in his early twenties, leans forward and yells. "Rosales you dumb shit! With his head up his ass, how could the Cap even hear Valdez?"

"Didn't you know, Adams? Valdez speaks asshole too!" laughs Rosales loudly.

Fucking Rosales is quick and funny, which you need in times like this. Regardless of how much training or experience you have, it's always a good thing to have a clown on board to add some levity to our miserable conditions. One time I was laughing so hard at Rosales' take on something offensive but funny, I couldn't drive and had to pull over to wipe away the tears so I could see where I was going.

A few nights ago, I had the strangest dream. I was trying to convince my friend to remember that we were two hundred and forty-five years old, but he wasn't accepting it. As much as I tried, he refused to believe we were that ancient. As for myself, it was the most wonderful feeling to have spent that many years on Earth. It was so clear, and I had detailed memories of events that were centuries old. I woke up so thrilled to have experienced over two centuries years of life—I was free of time.

The dream made me wonder if there's another reality we choose to ignore, probably because we haven't evolved enough to handle it. It's something to think about while staring at miles of nothing in front of me, because today I am back in the present and the past.

For miles, we've traveled through a countryside filled with ancient farmhouses and villages. On what little arable land there is, farmers are still using oxen much as they've done for centuries. It reminds me that it is us, me and my fellow Marines who have come from another time and place. We might as well be Martians, we're so different from these tribal people. Americans like to say that we should bring this country into the twenty-first century. I feel we could learn a lot by going back to the past because these folks aren't spewing carbon dioxide and poison all over the place—we are the ones doing that. Although bringing this place into the eighteenth century would be a giant leap from where they presently are, which is more like the fifteenth century.

The chatter quiets when we spot a wagon on the side of the road about a hundred yards away and I pull out the handset to instruct the others.

"Pay attention. Locals up ahead!"

"Fuck 'em!" yells Rosales, "lock and load!" overreacting as usual. Still, there's nothing wrong with being prepped, so I slow down to a cautious pace and observe a young local on the side of the road beside his donkey with a firm grip on the reins. I see he's got his hands full trying to calm his nervous animal who is freaked out by our noisy war machines. The young local keeps hold of the reins and walks to the cart—no aggressiveness to his gait, and stands protectively in front of a woman passenger sitting in the cart. I'm at ease watching him—nothing so far to indicate he will strike out.

The woman looks up and slowly turns her head to me. I'm shocked to find such an extraordinarily beautiful young woman in the middle of nowhere. I quickly surmise that she's no peasant either as she's wearing a very fine and expensive-looking tunic and dress. I can't help but notice too, her large green eyes outlined in black liner.

I'm transfixed, which is not cool in a situation until the spell is broken when a necklace with a gold crucifix glimmering in the bright sun and I blink out of my trance. The girl quickly covers the crucifix along with her face when the dust storm we've created catches up to us and chokes out the clear air.

We're not here to fight Christians, and the young man is no threat to us either. But the rest of my guys aren't feeling it.

"Min ayin atyt? (Where are you coming from?") I ask him in Arabic.

The young man tilts his head, puzzled by the words.

I find it strange that he doesn't speak Arabic and try speaking to him in English. "Where are you coming from?"

We are not understanding each other, but he is also not afraid of us either, only confused. Without any warning, the young man breaks into a wide smile, closes his eyes, and lifts his head skyward as if in prayer.

Rosales and the others begin yelling, "Valdez! He's gonna blow his ass up! They're fucking insurgents! Shoot him!"

Insurgents? Not this couple. I yell at Rosales, "This guy is all about love and peace you fuck head! Stand down!"

I put the vehicle in gear and moved out. "Learn some body language, idiots."

"What the shit, Valdez!"

Rosales leans past me and yells out my window.

191

"Onward Christian fucking soldiers!"

"Asshole!" I curse and push him back into his seat.

I lean out my window for another look but they've vanished into the past behind a veil of blinding dust. I turn back to the road ahead and step on the gas a little more firmly than I would have liked, but it snaps my guys back to the present and out of their war frenzy. Hopefully, my quick impression of the young couple is correct. Like many people of the desert, most are simply trying to live their lives like everyone else and unfortunately find themselves caught up in a war not of their own making.

Right now my guys are too eager to start something, and it has me worried. Our mission is to rescue hostages and make it back safely. I am not prepared to start slaughtering innocent civilians just because they appear to be from the time of Jesus.

THE END OF TIMES

I walk through the courtyard of Mark and Christine's house admiring their many potted citrus trees and Christine's impressive collection of succulents. At the double-wide wooden entry doors, I push on a stainless steel doorbell with an intercom. It seems a little out of place given the old-world feel of the courtyard, but probably necessary as the walls of the house are at least three feet thick.

"Hey David, come on in," says Christine over the speaker. I hear the door unlock with a quiet click and step inside. A soft breeze greets me in the foyer—the architect's energy-efficient floor plan to cool the house using cross-flow ventilation. It works for me and lends a calmness to the house. I take notice of my painting Jesus, the Teenage Years hanging all alone, with no danger to anyone. I can't help but stare at it for a bit, something I do every time I come up here and it seems to be getting better looking with age. I wonder what the vandals or vandals are up to these days because they went to a lot of trouble, not to mention arrest by leaving their message of protest on my art.

Mark enters and catches me staring at Teenage Jesus. "Have regrets about parting with your little masterpiece?"

"I do miss my painting. I don't remember it looking this good."

"It's always looked fantastic, that's why we bought it."

"Yes, now I remember. So, what's the big secret you couldn't tell me over the phone?"

"We want to commission you!"

"Really, a painting?"

"Yes, a painting. What else do you know how to do?"

And I think to myself, that snide remark is going to cost you.

I take a look at Mark's spectacular house and make a mental note to charge them an appropriate amount this time around. Christine told me she insured Teenage Jesus for thirty-five thousand dollars, which I thought was a bit optimistic seeing as I had never sold anything over three thousand dollars, which was how much they paid for Teenage Jesus. I mentioned that to her but she said she wouldn't part with it for any less.

We shake hands to start the process and Mark exclaims, "Let's celebrate with some Champagne then!"

Suddenly Christine bursts into the foyer raving about some news on the television. "Guys, get in here! You have to see this! Some religious nuts are holed up in a church. I think it's going to be another Waco or Ruby Ridge!"

She rushes back to the television room with us following as ordered. Upon entering the room, we see the image of an excited reporter filling the large flat-screen television. The graphic below the reporter reads, Hilltop Calvary Church, Pine Valley, Idaho.

I sit on the edge of the couch for a closer look as the camera pulls back to reveal a small, single-story wood-frame church. Dozens of police cars and emergency vehicles fill a gravel parking lot.

"We're going to take a chance and talk to Reverend Eugene Cranston, pastor of the First Church of Christ," says the reporter. He motions for the cameraman to follow him to the front door.

"Oh my God!" I laugh. "This is the guy who complained about me in the paper! Remember? I have his letter to the editor pasted on my refrigerator! Wow! Now I should frame it"

Mark and Christine turn to me in unison and ask, "What did you say? You know this guy?"

"Yes! He's one of the nut cases who has threatened me with eternal damnation to hell."

"Has he done it yet?" jokes Christine.

"Unless I repent for creating the unholy image of a teenage Jesus, I'm pretty sure I'm still be on his hit list. I can't believe this is the same guy!"

The reporter turns to the camera and moves in close to the lens, lowering his voice as he tells us in a conspiratorial tone, "I'm going to knock on the door and hopefully we'll get a word from the reverend."

Just before the reporter can reach up and knock, Reverend Cranston swings the door wide open. He's dressed in a white short-sleeve shirt and black slacks and stands with his hands on his hips staring at the reporter with a serious frown of disapproval.

The reporter stumbles back a step or two before recovering and asking, "Father Cranston, it's been reported that you and your congregation have been collecting weapons in preparation for some kind of doomsday. Do you care to comment?"

"I am not the Father! There is only one Father and He resides in heaven. I am not a priest either, mister. I preach and give counsel to those seeking salvation through the teachings of the Son of God, Jesus Christ."

"I see," nods the reporter, " Could you tell us then, what events triggered today's altercation with local authorities?"

Reverend Cranston hisses, "Drugs, promiscuity, premarital sex, abortion, homosexuality—an army of devil worshiping sinners if you don't already know. Report that to your listeners and inform them to get down on their knees and pray for salvation! The storm is gathering...the End of Times is upon us!"

The reporter turns to the camera with a nervous smile as Reverend Cranston continues his rant. "The day of the Lord will come like a thief. Your dead shall live; their bodies shall rise. You who dwell in the dust, awake and sing for joy! For your dew is a dew of light, and the earth will give birth to the dead. That day will bring about the destruction of the heavens by fire, and the elements will melt in the heat."

The reporter continues nodding while patiently waiting for a break in the sermon. Finally, Reverend Cranston has to take a breath and stops talking long enough for the reporter to ask, "Is it true that you've sent out hit squads to bomb mosques, Planned Parenthood clinics, and critics of your hellfire and brimstone sermons?"

Reverend Cranston takes a step closer to the camera and lifts his arms to the sky. "Do I take any pleasure that the wicked should die? Do you say the way of the Lord is not fair? Repent then, and turn away from all your transgressions, so that iniquity will not be your ruin! Lamentations 3,4!"

Christine grabs the remote and mutes the sound on the television. "Champagne, anyone?"

She has three filled glasses on a tray and lays it down on the coffee table and hands me a glass. "To a new painting!" she cheers and we raise our glasses and toast, "Salute!"

Mark asks me, "Do you think that guy has seen the poster of Teenage Jesus? The one you've been selling to gullible defenseless teenagers?"

"I wouldn't doubt that he knows all about Teenage Jesus and the unrepentant sinner who created it. It's idiots like this guy and his band of zealots that probably had something to do with poor Teenage Jesus over there getting tagged."

"We're lucky he didn't send out a hit squad to find you. You know, he might have discovered that we bought the painting and could firebomb our house!" exclaims Mark.

"Wow, it would really been valuable then," I laugh.

"No, seriously, David."

"Calm down, Mark. Whatever he's up to now has nothing to do with that painting. I think you should seriously worry about him discovering that you're hiring me to paint more blaspheming art."

Mark's occasional flare-ups of angst are always followed by his excellent sense of humor. "I hope he's wrong about the end of the world, I've got a new piece of property I'm developing!"

"I am so sick of Jesus freaks," I complain. "They take all the fun out of everything. Jesus preached tolerance, but there's been nothing but trouble ever since the church got hold of his words and screwed them all up. Where's the love?"

Christine raises her glass. "I'll drink to that!"

We turn our heads when the front door opens and slams shut. The sound of sandals flip-flopping on the tile floor grows louder as Mimi enters the television room and collapses on a chair. She stares blankly at the television and does not attempt to conceal that she's been crying. She wipes tears from her cheeks and eyes and asks, "What's going on?"

Mark replies, "There's a bunch of religious crazies in a stand-off with the ATF, or the FBI."

"Really?" she sniffles.

"What's wrong honey?" asks Christine.

Mimi inhales deeply and exhales, "The end of the world, that's what. Tim's back in Iraq! There's some big problem, and he had to haul ass back to the base. He barely had time to say goodbye!"

Mimi covers her face with her hands before jumping up and running up the stairs toward her old bedroom. "It's not right!" she cries, "He's already been there!"

"Oh shit. Poor kid," says Christine as she grabs the remote and turns off the television. The Reverend's voice echoes about the room briefly before fading away to silence.

Mark puts his glass down. "I better go check on her."

"I thought she had her own place?" I ask.

"This must be bad," he replies with a concerned look on his face. He glances up in the direction of Mimi's bedroom and says, "She hasn't set foot in her room since she moved out."

Mark puts his ear to the door and can hear Mimi crying softly. He knocks quietly and asks, "Mimi? Are you all right?"

"I'm okay, Dad. Tim's house just felt so lonely and I needed to be here with family. You don't mind, do you?"

"Not at all. I understand, sweetie, and if you need anything, let us know, okay? I love you."

"I love you too, Dad."

Stretched out on the bed staring at the ceiling, Mimi is thinking about Tim and how his presence in her life has changed her so much. She finds it hard to believe that she ran back home to Mom and Dad for one thing, but it is good to have a place of refuge when things head south. She laughs when she looks around her old room, the place she sought sanctuary in, which features posters of punk bands and surfing, but there's also a large framed photograph of her with a half dozen Mayan women in colorful dresses.

Mimi closes her eyes and curls into a fetal position and holds her hands tightly in prayer, pressing them tightly against her lips and letting the tears flow freely. "Dear God. Please God. Watch over Tim and protect him. I love him so much...I love him so much."

Judas is kneeling on a stack of blankets and boxed goods with his head between us, keeping us entertained with his odd views about the world we live in.

"God has said that five Israelites can slay fifty enemies. If this is true, and I believe it to be so, why are we unable to be rid of them? We remove fifty of them from this life and one hundred more show up in their place! They breed like locusts," he laughs.

It has been an uneventful journey into these mountains, and it has given me time to think about what I will find in Bethlehem. My thoughts are distracting and it bothers me as they take me from enjoying Mary and Judas' company.

"Judas, you might never be able to return," says Mary. "If the Romans recognize you, it is death. You know that, right?"

Judas scoffs. "We all look the same to these invaders. Anyway, I am not running away from anything. Is it not obvious that God had directed me to you? These mountains are full of bandits, and a lot of good the Romans are, our so-called 'liberators.' What have they liberated us from except from our land? Wiping them off the face of the earth can only benefit the rest of humanity."

I slow the cart when I hear a thunderous storm growing louder in the distance.

"Why are you slowing?" asks Judas.

"Quiet down! I hear something," I order.

I hear a deep rumbling accompanied by a large cloud of dust heading toward us beyond a hill we're about to pass over. Without delay, I pull the wagon off to the side.

"Quickly! Get under cover!" I shout.

"Why? What is happening?" asks Judas.

"Dust storm and it looks enormous"

Judas finally notices the approaching cloud and the roar, and jumps in the back, burying himself deep under the supplies. Mary helps further by covering him with more goods. The increasing clamor is also making the donkey jittery and frightened and fighting the beast takes all my strength to keep him from bolting.

Mary grabs a blanket from under the seat and jumps to the ground and grabs the animal by the bridle, then quickly places the blanket over his eyes to calm him and keep him still. She does this just in time as the violent storm is upon us.

Mary races back to the cart and we cover ourselves also and curl up on the seat. I take her hand squeeze it tightly and shout over the noise "Hold on!"

We brace for a lashing from the sand kicked up by the force of the winds but are surprised when there is none. Only thick, choking dust swirling around us that I fear will bring about our deaths. More frightening is the deafening roar of the storm's fury like the sound of the Roman war machines. Deep within the chaos, I hear the wind cursing us in a language I do not understand. "Aire u omen fren?" It repeats the chant two or three more times, "Aire u omen fren?"

The storm has passed and I crawl out from under the blanket and see the backside of the storm with a long trail of dust obediently following it like the tail of a serpent.

Mary extracts herself from under the bench and uncovers her face, looks around nervously, then, almost laughing exclaims, "That was a most frightening and unusual event!"

I take her hand when she jumps into my awaiting arms, and we both begin laughing, not only because we survived a frightening experience, but also because of our dust-covered appearance. Tears of laughter create muddy streaks on our faces, which only makes us laugh even more.

We gather our wits and brush off our clothing, then stop when we hear a muffled cry from deep beneath the blankets and run to the back of the wagon. "Judas!" we call out in unison.

Wasting no time, we begin digging out our friend from under blankets covered in dust. Once unearthed, Judas jumps to the ground and laughs. "Great heavens! That was a hellish storm. I thought we were about to be trampled by demons. What kind of storm was that?"

The language I heard in the dust felt as if it was from another world, and I shudder that we might never be free of the Romans or people like them.

I asked Mary if she saw anything unusual in the dust.

"My eyes were closed. It was so terrifying!" she says. "I felt as though the ground might rise up and throw us into the canyon."

I think about the ancient texts I buried myself in as a young boy and searched my memory for an explanation. According to Greek mythology, life is a stage where we are toyed with and tormented by the Gods for their enjoyment. Many discovered in ancient ruins examples that some of these myths were not as far-fetched as one might imagine.

Judas looks about the landscape utterly confused. Whatever it was has left no evidence of having ever existed other than the vast amounts of dust we are covered in.

"It is the end of days," he remarks.

The following morning breaks with a clear sky, relief for

three weary travelers who spent the night wrapped in blankets, huddled under the cart when dark clouds traveling across the plain had their progress halted when they slammed into the mountains surrounding us. Angered by this interruption, they spewed bolts of lightning followed by ear-splitting claps of thunder throughout the night. Fortunately for us, we were spared any rain. At daybreak, the storm passed over the peaks and rewarded us with a magnificent and breathtaking sunrise.

We journeyed through a landscape of rocky hills before the road brought us to a long, gentle valley to the village of Bethlehem perched on the edge of a cliff with a crumbling wall spilling over the side. Despite this, it overlooked a well-maintained vineyard and orchards filled with olive and fruit trees.

A shepherd's dog barks out a warning of our approach, spooking the grazing sheep who bolt for a very short distance before the dog races off to block their movement. Our sudden appearance also surprises a few townspeople repairing a small section of fence who stop their work and stare at us in wonder.

As we walk alongside the cart Judas stops and asks, "How do you think we will fare with these people?"

I glance up to the village and see a few small figures peering down at us and reply, "There is no way of predicting where things will go from here"

Judas shakes his head as he studies the village. "This town is a dump on a pile of rubble."

The town does look to be struggling, and it saddens me to think that the greatness they hoped for never came. Wise men dwell here, I was told by Mother. Maybe so, but prosperity it seems, has bypassed this town. It is entirely possible that the men I seek may not even be here, having either died or left many years ago. The atmosphere feels illusory, a dream as I walk by the side of Mary at the place of my birth. I wonder momentarily if I am still lying unconscious in the alley from the blow I received. The old physician called this state a koma—the deep sleep. Mary touches my arm softly, an unspoken reply that lovers do almost unconsciously when they see their partner struggling. I am awake then, as no dream would conjure the feeling of warmth or tenderness of her touch.

"Judas and I will stay here," she tells me. "You go to the village and decide if this is what you desire."

Mary sadly shakes her head while looking at the ruinous state of the barns and broken fences and says, "They are certainly in need of our help."

I look at the same desperate landscape and reply, "They truly are, and I am in need of theirs."

I climb the pathway, unsure of what I will find, but still willing, that is, until I enter the little village of Bethlehem. The town square is well-maintained, but it appears that many of its buildings are in a weakened state. The well in the center of town jolts my memory, and I recall the many trips with my mother to fetch water and listen to the women exchange greetings and talk. Beyond the well is a small temple, and near it, I see what looks to be a small circular mausoleum or crypt. As I near the building, my chest tightens, and for good reason, too. I read a small sign over the entrance carved with twenty-five names of those entombed within because a bright star appeared seventeen years earlier.

The mausoleum draws me inside almost against my will, but I cautiously enter. The dark room is lit by a single oil lamp, its smoke lazily floating upward through a hole in the roof acting as a vent. When my eyes grow accustomed to the darkness, I look down at the floor of hand-cut stones and count twenty-five that circle the lamp. My legs give way and I fall to my knees when my heart stops beating and I am unable to breathe.

I crawl on the floor like a child and touch every cold stone. At each one, I ask forgiveness from the boy buried beneath. There are no names carved into the stones but I know some would certainly have become my playmates. Their souls were freed when their lives ended while mine remains hidden away in a crypt of my own making, buried deep within my heart.

Emotions within burst forth and kicked me in the gut. I gasp, then begin to weep uncontrollably until I exhaust myself and fall into a deep sleep. In this sleep, glowing lights dance in patterns around the smoke, spinning wildly about my body. I hear a deep music, like a breeze lazily traveling through the forest, and I feel it must be the spirits of the children. They fill the room translucent as smoke, hovering over me and caressing me lightly. When their singing becomes faint I follow their voices and am sent into a world beyond light and without shape. All is deathly quiet until a voice calls out to me in a whisper.

"Can you hear me? I have rested here so long I thought myself to be dead."

I ask myself, "Am I dreaming?" I scan the blackness searching for a shape, but see nothing but blackness.

The voice asks, "Why have you traveled to this tomb?"

I have no answer.

"What do you seek here?"

"Who are you?" I ask.

"I am the one you locked away."

"Because of those children."

"You committed no crime here."

"They died because of me."

"I ask again, what do you seek here?"

"Forgiveness … knowledge … truth."

"For what you have been seeking, you already know."

I open my eyes to light and wonder how long I have slept. I crawl to the small doorway and peer out to see that the shadow of the old olive tree has crossed the square and the temperature has grown cool—it must be nearing late afternoon. I roll onto my back knowing what I suspected when I arrived in this village that such an experience might be waiting for me, but always afraid it might.

Sleep leaves me and I become aware of a lightness of spirit, as though I have been cleansed. Rarely have I felt such a profound sense of ease—one might even say I am even happy. I offer a simple prayer to the children, thank them for their song, and I ask once again for forgiveness and promise to honor their deaths and strive to become a better person.

At the center of the square is a bench under the large olive tree and I take a seat. Shortly, I am met by an Elder, and without speaking he takes my hand and leads me to the low wall overlooking the valley.

"What a pleasant surprise it is that you have returned to us. We have always prayed that you might."

"You are the Village Elder known as Eron?"

He offers me a kind smile, his eyes twinkling as he tells me, "I see you are still able to remember every memory and story told to you."

I nod in agreement, "At times it is a curse. Every event, joyful or sad, is as if it happened only moments ago."

"That is a burden indeed," he says. "Still, such an awareness at an early age gave us strong evidence that you were....well, that you were very special."

"I remembered everything told to me but lacked the words to express my feelings. How is it that you know it is me?"

Eron laughs. "I am not a magician! You were in the tomb for a very long time. Your young wife and friend told us of your journey and have already made arrangements for lodging. Come, they are gathering up your belongings."

As we walk to the village gate, Eron asks, "Are you prepared to face your accuser?"

"My accuser?" I ask in surprise.

"A child much like yourself. One of your playmates."

"I thought all were killed?"

"His mother saved him, praise God. Sadly, some cast blame, accusing her of losing faith which angered God, thus leaving us unprotected from Herod's soldiers."

"How could anyone believe such a thing?"

"Such is the way of grief," he smiles. "Time has healed those wounds. And yourself? Who do you blame?"

I almost stumble at his words. "You are wise, but I no longer blame anyone."

I see a crowd has surrounded Mary and Judas and is assisting them in carrying packages to our new lodging. I also notice that a few young women have become enthralled with Mary. They touch her finely crafted skirt and shawl and hold her hands as they walk.

A strong young man carrying one of Mary's chests looks our way and nods a greeting. Eron waves the man over and says, "This young man is Matthew."

"He is the other survivor?" I as

k.

"Yes, he is. Much like you I suspect, he spent much of his life asking the Father why only he survived while the others perished, but no answer was ever given to ease his pain. Like many in Bethlehem, we have learned to quiet the voice, allowing it to walk beside us without affecting our travel. I am certain all will be revealed at the proper moment. In Matthew's case, he was the one who built the crypt for the children and through his labors released his suffering which is a malignancy."

Matthew stops his work and studies me as walks over to us.

Will Matthew attack me? I wonder.

Eron asks him, "What do you have to say to the son of Joseph and Mary?"

I notice a large scar running across his neck—his life spared when his mother, as any mother would, rescued him from danger.

I think of my father who taught me a trade and the skills to build shelter for our people, and my uncle whose ships gave me a view of the greater world.

One of the sailors I traveled with was aware of my religious training, and laughed as we were pulling in a large number of fish caught in our nets. "Do you see this young Rabbi? See the great fish of the sea and how they struggle against our nets and the hooks? Do they not also display characteristics that look like courage and tenacity? How does one decide that only we have the holy spark and the fish does not?" It was a simple lesson, not from a man of learning, but from a man who lived with nature.

I have met many people who had a great awareness of life. All of it it turns out, was a path I was on without even realizing it. Those were not idle years where my education suffered, but a time when I learned more about the world than had I lived in a sanctuary buried in religious texts. Bethlehem has waited for a reply to their sacrifice for many years, and I still wonder if I will be welcomed as a friend, or will my fellow survivor slap me in anger. I brace myself for his response to my presence.

"This is a most blessed day," says Matthew, and he embraces me with a warm hug. "What would you have us do?"

I think, *explain to me why we miraculously survived while our innocent playmates did not.*

Surviving comes with a price—a sense of responsibility for having played a role in the killings.

I ask Matthew about the condition of the town. "I am curious why the orchards are so well-cared for, yet many buildings are in a sad state of disrepair. It makes no sense."

"We lost our best craftsmen when they were ordered to work on the Great Temple in Jerusalem. We have tried, but my crypt for the children is about the only structure that hasn't collapsed."

Eron asks, "Your father was a fine carpenter; do you possess any of his skills?"

"Yes, I believe I can be of great help."

"Then, it is settled," beams Eron. "We shall make the little town of Bethlehem once again a beacon of light."

THE WAR IS OVER

The mountainous terrain toward our goal offered us an endless series of dirt roads curving around ridges that it seem as though we were doubling back on ourselves. After a long day of this, we are deposited into a fertile valley filled with well-tended wheat fields interlaced with canals built more than two thousand years earlier. An ancient walled city a mile away looms large over the flat plain, with its intimidating massive stone walls giving us pause and a tightening in the gut. Iraq is called the "Cradle of Civilization" and this city is certainly evidence of that, probably built by Sumerians or Babylonians in an age of flying carpets and jinnis.

Sadly, there are some of my comrades who would like to blow the shit out of this world's treasure to rescue three French doctors.

Rosales shouts, "I think we found Oz!"

"We're sure as shit not in Kansas anymore," laughs Adams.

"Valdez, whadaya gonna do?" asks Rosales.

"Halt this parade first thing," I say. "Man, that is one impressive structure."

"Let's get closer and find out what the situation is. See if the Wizard will open the gate for us or if the Wicked Witch is still in control," laughs Adams.

"I say stay put and let them come to us," says Rosales. "We'll be sitting ducks down there."

"You might be right. Let me think for a minute," I tell them.

We can't move forward, that's for certain. Presently, we're out of range of most rocket launchers, but I don't want to test my assumption to find out if they have any. I pull out my binoculars and study the situation when I see the gates open and two well-dressed men step out into the noonday sun waving a large white flag, or possibly a white bed sheet. I think they might be tribal leaders or the mayor.

"Valdez, they've got a white flag!" says Rosales.

"No shit."

I pick up the mic and tell the rest of the convoy to stand pat while we meet these guys halfway. It's a slow ride and an ambush is still a strong possibility. I go as far as I consider safe and wait for the Iraqis to move closer to our vehicle. Despite the ancient pattern of feuding tribes, and most recently, radical jihadists, the average Iraqi is warm and hospitable.

One of the men, the apparent leader of the group greets me with a bow. "As-salaam alaykum wa rahmatullahi wa barakaatuhu."

"As-salaam alaykum," I reply. "Ma esmouk? (What is your name?)"

"Esmee Al Tayyib," he says, and I hope it's true—Al Tayyib means "the good one" in Arabic.

He tells me in broken English that the hostages have been treated well and are unharmed. They got trapped in this town after a short but intense battle and the rebels were defeated and run out of the city by the local militia.

I ask him in Arabic, "Where have they fled to?"

As much as I try to speak his language, he continues talking to me in English, a sign of respect to be sure, but I don't think speaking English flies with the jihadists.

Al Tayyib continues, "Many of them had farms to be tended to. Others I believe, scattered to regroup after suffering so many casualties. They will not attack this city again, but I cannot promise you that they will not try to attack you on the road."

I see Al Tayyib's eyes begin darting to the right and left toward the wheat fields—a silent communication telling me where the enemy is hiding

I nod once and ask, "Where are the hostages?"

"They are in good spirits and are ready to journey with you," replies Al Tayyib. He lowers his voice and says, "Please hurry."

"Get them out here now." I radio back to the convoy to move forward a half-klick, lock, and load, and prepare for some shit.

I thank Al Tayyib and he quickly scurries back to the gates where he nervously signals with quick hand movements to someone inside the city.

Shortly the three hostages walk out and Al Tayyib ushers them a dozen yards from the walls, almost shoving them away from the gates. He watches the hostages until they near us then turns and races back to safety behind the gate. Once he's inside, the gate quickly drops to the ground, its massive iron chains make a thunderous racket against the metal pulleys, and hit the ground with a thunderous explosion. This is followed by an uncomfortable silence that ends any hope I had of this day proceeding without a major problem.

Upon hearing the gates slam shut, the three hostages—two men and a woman, freeze in their tracks ten yards from the safety of our vehicle. I yell at them, "Get in, get the hell in!"

Rosales and Adams jump out and pick the men up by their arms, followed by the female hostage, and throw them into the vehicle. At the same time, I run to the Humvee and step on it. I do a world-class donut while pounding on the steering wheel, begging the beast to come to life and move out before the shit hits the fan.

We are completely vulnerable and far from effective support. Time grinds to a halt and now everything begins happening in slow motion even though we're moving at hyper speed. If you don't take advantage of this phenomenon you are toast. If fear takes over and you hesitate, you may wind up dead, and right now is not a good time to be afraid. The attack came less than a fifty meters from the gate as we raced back to the convoy.

"Ali Baba on the left!" screams Adams.

"Get your fucking heads down!" I yell when I see a dozen men emerge from the wheat fields and begin lighting us up.

I concentrate on getting us as far away from the ambush as possible. Dust is exploding off the vehicle from bullets as the rapid-fire begins hitting us. The armor plating survives as do the recently installed window kits—completely useless because Rosales and Adams have to roll them down to fire back. The rear right window explodes and covers the hostages in high-tech plastic and whatever else those things are made of.

I'm hit with a clod of a hardball-sized chunk of dirt that hits me squarely in the ear. I'm cleaning out my ear when I hear our support coming in hot with their powerful weapons echoing throughout the valley with an ear-splitting, "thump, thump, thump." Our guys up the road reacted swiftly to the ambush and are now fully engaged.

Rapid-fire is hitting us from all directions. Debris begins raining down onto our roof with a terrible din. I hear screaming from the back seat, but when I turn around I nearly begin laughing when I see it's not the woman as I falsely presumed. She has assumed the correct posture and has her head tucked between her legs. It's the two male doctors sitting straight up in their seats crying, "Nous allons mourir! (we're going to die!")

Our artillery is effectively mowing down innocent stacks of wheat stalks and insurgents like a giant John Deere thresher. In less than thirty seconds it's all over, and that's the end of modern warfare just outside the walls ancient world of Babylon.

"Everyone accounted for?" I ask although my head is in a fog. I can't see the raod clearly now, so I take my foot off the gas and come to a halt.

"Hey, you okay Valdez?"

I hear a muted voice growing fainter. "Valdez, are you okay? Shit, stay awake, dude! Stay awake!"

I don't remember much of anything on the drive back to the base except when I think I was looking out the window and saw a young dark man and Mimi with their cart parked on the side of the road. The man was holding his arms high in the air and laughing hysterically, even though explosions were going off all around him. I saw Mimi holding a photograph of us in her parent's garden and she had tears streaming down her cheeks and I heard her voice over the bombs repeating the words, "I love you," over and over. I felt helpless that I couldn't let her know I was okay because I was tied down on a bed. The vision ended when they disappeared into the dust and I guess I lost consciousness after that.

Thankfully, our hostages kept me alive and I'm glad I wasn't a witness to the procedure—a tubal thoracostomy to drain blood and other fluids from my chest. A bullet had hit my door and managed to make it past the exterior panel sending some shrapnel into my left lung only an inch from my heart. I was so out of it, that I don't even remember the plane flight when I got transported to Germany where the doctors fixed me up.

Two months ago I received my separation papers and an honorable discharge from the Marines, including a standard letter thanking me for my service. I also got a bottle of expensive wine and a sweet letter from the doctors thanking me for rescuing them. I'll have to write back and thank them for saving my life too.

When I made it back home, the doctors advised me to begin a robust regimen of exercise to strengthen my heart and build up my lungs. It was excellent advice that meant I would be able to surf again—doctor's orders.

Mimi joined me on my daily run through the park, at a snail's pace at first, but soon turned into a good healthy sprint up the hill where we would stop at a bench under a giant redwood tree to catch our breath and enjoy the city views. One morning I looked up and saw an arrow ten feet above us stuck in the trunk. "Mimi, check it out! That's an arrow from a crossbow! You know those things are dangerous if you're not a professional"

I didn't know if Mimi knew much about crossbows, but I saw plenty of them in Iraq. Not every insurgent has an automatic weapon or a grenade launcher—arrows kill people too, and are a lot quieter.

Mimi shook her head and laughed, "Whatever this idiot was aiming at, I doubt they mised by a mile!"

I had a mild case of PTSD from getting blasted. Nothing serious, just a little depression. It didn't last long once I began surfing again. One day while I was sitting in the linep waiting for a wave , I thought if surfing could snap me out of my funk, maybe it could work for other vets, so I hooked up with a couple of my buddies from Iraq and asked them if they wanted to take up surfing. . The guys were hesitant at first because they had never ventured beyond the soup. "Think of it as a day of fun in tiny little waves. It'll be fun, trust me."

After an hour of flaying about in the ocean, an hour into the session the magic happened—they were standing up and cruising toward shore in the soup howling with joy. They wanted more, and they became hooked as most do. Within weeks the war and its residual damage began to fade away.

One of my buddies told his shrink at the VA about our surfing and how it made him feel—like his PTSD wasn't bothering him as much, and that it might work for other veterans. The VA clinic was open to anything that might help the soldiers and interviewed me to make sure it wasn't a scam. When I passed muster, they set me up for a meeting with the Commanding Officer at Pendleton.

In the meantime, I discovered there was research being done by UCLA doctors who were touting the benefits of the ocean. When I presented this information during my interview, the Commander asked me to volunteer at first because he didn't know what my job classification should be.

"Valdez," he finally decided, "how about we just make you a lifeguard until we figure something out."

It took us a couple of months to get everything and everybody on board and ready for our first session. It strikes me as odd how my life has turned out; I'm in love with a beautiful girl who feels the same way about me, and six months after nearly dying in Iraq, I surf for a living by conducting surfing classes for war veterans at a private beach break on the base.

THE DUMP
ON A PILE OF RUBBLE

Mary and I settled into a spacious room at the inn while we searched the area for housing. It was not long before we located an abandoned farm close to the village and began making it livable. Judas is also repairing an old barn on the property, although he is restless and I doubt he will remain with us for very long.

I sent a messenger to the shop in Joppa for needed supplies and a short time later, Yaron and Sarah arrived with a wagon filled with clothing, tools, and a large supply of medicinal supplies such as oils, herbs, and healing cloths. Also included was the gift of a large barrel of healing water, courtesy of Uncle Joseph, who wrote us to say that commerce had returned to the old port, but a gathering of five or more people was still illegal and quickly scattered by soldiers.

I hike the hills surrounding Bethlehem and find the land to be a treasure chest of edible wild flora including many plants containing medicinal properties—Palestine oak, terebinth for ridding the body of lice, and when rubbed on the body with palm oil, as a lineament for breathing or sore throat problems. The aloe plant is plentiful and is an excellent treatment for burns. When taken internally, it purges the stomach and relieves fevers. Golden chamomile and stinkbush protect open wounds from further infection.

A spring pours from the rocks above the village, one of many that are a source of water filling our wells and irrigating the fields. It is also where I stop for a refreshing pause to catch my breath from the climb and the spring is a good place to take time to meditate. About this time I usually become aware of the aroma of stews and freshly baked bread that fills the air and calls me home.

Shortly after we arrived in Bethlehem, Mary began taking Bethlehem's products such as lemons and oranges, grapes, cheese, and wine, to the huge market in Jerusalem. Her experience running her father's estate was an important skill for the trading of goods and has enriched Bethlehem with much-needed coin.

Following her first trip to Jerusalem, Mary told me of the most horrific living conditions and the multitude of poor beggars, much worse than in Joppa, so I accompanied Mary on her next visit. What I saw long before we reached the famous gates of the city, we passed through an endless gauntlet of the poor, the sick, and the insane lining the road. The magnitude of such poverty was beyond anything I had thought possible and I recalled the words of one of my teachers: "For every man who gains wealth, one hundred sinks into poverty."

Jerusalem is the holiest site for Hebrews and is also a magnet for religious zealots. Many are touched by a hand only they can see, and believe themselves to be saints or messiahs. Amongst the poor and sick lining the roads these holy men also have their hands out, offering prayers and salvation for a price, although if a coin is not given, they curse you with eternal damnation. When the day is done, the poor and sick return to the slums that surround the city, so populous and massive they dwarf Jerusalem by a hundredfold.

The Great Temple, the pride of the Jerusalem, overlooks this sea of humanity and has been under construction for close to seventy years. Despite Herod's death, his son, also known as Herod, continued with his father's dream of eternal glory. The steady work meant that many had abandoned their farms to work at the temple. Unfortunately, if they were injured or their trade was no longer required, they would find themselves without land, or hope.

Many years ago, Jerusalem took great care of its citizens with fine clinics and sanctuaries for the destitute. These services were supported by taxes, but today the Temple's building costs have bankrupted the coffers of the king and the church. The Golden Temple is a farce; a monument to Herod, the King who murdered twenty-five children because he was afraid of losing power.

When I stood at the entrance of the Temple's East Gate, never before had I wished that I truly was the one my mother prayed for—the one who would put an end to disease, poverty, and pain, and bring peace and equity to our people.

When she was not busy, Mary would accompany me on my forays into the hills. One afternoon at my favorite spring, we stopped to rest. I placed a blanket on the ground, and Mary uncovered a basket filled with a spread of dried fruit, bread, and cheese.

As she prepared the food, Mary asked, "Do you remember when you said that nature hides itself?"

"Of course," I replied. "It was when I was searching for the stinkbush."

"It struck me as an interesting parable. In all things, man included, we hide our true nature."

Her perceptive interpretation aroused my interest and gave me thought. It is true that gold and silver are hidden deep within the earth, but also, some of the most valuable and useful objects can be found upon the surface; crystals, amber, myrrh and frankincense—

all is here if one only looks.

"Do you feel I hid my true nature?" I replied.

She smiled at me and touched my hand. "Less so every day. You are a golden treasure, my love."

"Many search for gold," I replied. "They spend their lives digging much earth but most find very little reward,"

Mary laughed and kissed my hand. "But we have the rest of our lives to at least try."

On another venture into the hills, I was accompanied by Matthew, and he brought up the subject of the children.

"If you want to ask me about them, the innocents..." he said quietly before his voice trailed off.

"There is much I have wanted to know, Matthew. I was not certain of your feelings, but I am glad you brought up the subject."

"Ask me anything. I will keep nothing hidden."

"I am curious how were you treated by the townspeople." I ask. "Neighbors who were not only friends but relatives too. Were they not angry at your mother, and you, for having survived while their children died?"

"It is strange, but friends and family never wavered in their faith. I do not remember any of the children, and my wounds kept me in poor health for some time. As I grew in age, I did suffer. I sensed that all eyes were cast in my direction, that having lived, maybe it was me who was destined for greatness. Although I do not know what was expected of me."

"I believe we suffered together in that regard," I say.

"It was not until I began work on the crypt that I began to understand that we must live a life grounded in truth. The elders said the memorial was my calling, and as it turned out, it was my healing process too."

"It is a remarkable structure," I say.

"During construction, I sensed their presence, you know. "

This stuns me; one does not converse with the dead. I have not even told Mary of my experience in the tomb.

"It is a peaceful sanctuary for me," he adds. "I find it is simply a place where I can talk."

"To the children?" I ask.

"No, no, although at one time I felt I might have been able to. I do not consider the building a tomb or a mausoleum, but more of a retreat where I might converse with God. Whether He hears me or not I do not know, but confession is good."

I asked him if the people of Bethlehem felt betrayed by the vision of my father and the angel who warned him in a dream.

"How could they be when his dream was true? The soldiers did come."

Once again my anger clouded my thinking and affected my behavior. It is true then—my father's dream foretold of a horrible event that did come to the village.

I realize that Matthew's invitation to talk about the killings is as much for him as it is for me. He continues, "The lesson the elders teach is one of forgiveness. We pray that our path is a righteous one, and so far, our faith has kept us from further harm or persecution. The soldiers have never returned even though their mission failed, and Herod is dead. We are shunned by some who do not understand how the people of Bethlehem allowed the tragedy to unfold. And that has affected us to some degree, but we live in peace."

"Forgiveness is your weapon then," I answer.

"Forgiveness is followed by a joyful life," says Matthew.

Matthew changes the subject and says, "There is a girl who lives in Shiloh. We do not know each other well, but my family feels she would make a good partner and have arranged a marriage contract. We are waiting for the harvest to end before the joining of our families.

I wish I could say something about the importance of also having a loving partner, but it is not my place.

Unable to sleep, I wake Mary with my stirring and she pulls me to her and asks, "Is there something wrong? Are you troubled?"

"I cannot sleep," I reply. "Forgive me for waking you."

Mary sighs, "Tell me what bothers you."

I reply, "I have wanted to tell you about a vision or a dream I experienced from that storm the mountain road. I am not certain of its meaning, but I fear of what is to come. "

"Did you hear a creature in the dust?" she asks.

"You heard something too?" I joyfully ask.

Mary replies, "If that is what is was. It was a terrifying and most unnatural. Tell me what you heard."

I was so worried about my dream, I felt that it might frighten you and think that maybe you had married one touched by strange spirits.

Stumbling on my words at first, my mind races faster than the tongue. "I believe that what I heard might not be of this time. Maybe there is a wisdom within each of us that knows of vistas far beyond our ability to comprehend. Life as we are told is everything that is, was, and will be."

Mary nods in agreement and says, "Yes, the Creator completed his work in six days then rested on the seventh."

"If He created everything, might He not include time?

221

Imagine that time—past, present, and future is with us, just as much as the plants and the animals. If God created everything, is it only referring to the present moment, and does it only include the canopy of stars and the Earth we live on? Is there nothing else?"

Mary ponders this statement for a moment before answering, "I had never thought of time as an element of creation, but it is an exciting concept. You surprise me once again—my carpenter and physician, and also a philosopher. This is exciting. So what do you think we heard?"

"I am not certain. Maybe, for a brief moment, I glimpsed what is to come."

We are thrilled and haunted by this, but cannot draw any conclusions. Finally, I say, "In a world far beyond our land, maybe this kind of event is not such a rare thing."

"Why do you think it presented itself to you?" asks Mary.

"The storm was dark and warlike, and it puzzled me. I awoke feeling that faith in oneself is truly mightier than armor and swords because it did not destroy us."

"It seems that life is up to us alone," sighs Mary.

I gently rub her shoulders and reply, "Yes, but in a community of like minds. That is where success lies, of that I am certain."

Mary rests her head on my chest and words cannot express the joy I feel with her lying next to me even though my mind is filled with thoughts. I am surprised that Mary can sense my unease when she asks, "What other thoughts keep you awake?"

Sometimes what is in the mind is difficult to put into words. The easiest way to explain your thoughts can be with one word to begin with. "Creation," I say. "Is it not strange how a star plummets to earth as fire before turning to cold rock? Then, with the passage of time, turns to dust, picked up by the wind, and one day lands in an orchard to fertilize the soil. It is not what it began as, but it did not die either. It is as if life is everlasting."

"I have had this thought many times as I looked up to the stars over Magdala. I feel so relieved that you have these thoughts too," replies Mary. "I was worried you had married a troubled, mad woman."

"It appears we share the same dream," I whisper.

Mary nudges close and hugs me tighter. "Bethlehem is not to be our final destination, is it?"

"No, I do not think so," I reply.

"Jerusalem or beyond?" she asks.

"Either way," I say. "But I know for certain that you will find beyond very interesting."

"Are you interested in discovering more about the three Persian kings who came from the east?" Mary asks, "They traveled to Bethlehem because the stars told them of your birth, which I find fascinating as if this was possible."

"The stars do guide my uncle's ships to new lands across the vast seas. But the Persians' journey was in error as no king was born on that day."

"That is a story that has not yet been told," says Mary.

☙ ☙ ☙

"Are you planning on spending the rest of your life picking flowers and weeds?" Asks Judas while we're working on our small home. "I appreciate that you are a husband now with a spectacularly beautiful and intelligent wife, but are you truly content in this desolate outpost? Is this the end of the road for you?"

Judas has spent the past few weeks complaining to me about his life in Bethlehem. He is a fighter and there is no fight to be had here. The nature of this town, thanks to the efforts of the elders,

223

is one of community. All are equal and none live in splendor while another suffers because of illness or disability. What Judas fails to grasp is that while we have been helping them rebuild their village, we are planning to take our skills to other villages in need.

"You were never the fighter," says Judas. "You were great fun at mischief and mayhem, and you did plan many great escapades. But, I always knew that fighting was not in your heart."

My desire to be rid of the Romans is as real as his, but an armed struggle will only bring death and an end to the Jewish race. The Romans have ruled over us for two hundred years, and will not leave until their empire collapses and they are forced to return to Rome.

"I am not criticizing your efforts or this town. It is a charming spot to grow old in," continues Judas. "You are my dearest brother, and I cherish our friendship. I am simply stating a fact."

"Then, you are leaving?" I ask.

"You have seen Jerusalem," replies Judas. "There are a great many like me, revolutionaries and fighters who can use my skills."

"We may not be in Bethlehem for much longer, either. Mary and I want to continue this work in other villages, like what we have accomplished in Bethlehem."

"You are on the right course and you may bring peace before an armed struggle does. But as you know, that is not my way."

I nod in agreement. "If Jerusalem rejects your talents, we will still require a formidable fighter and ally on our journey."

Judas gives me a strong, emotional bear hug, then turns his away. He is not fooling me with his toughness, I saw his eyes welling up with tears. I am filled with joy to call him a friend and brother.

Judas is leaving for Jerusalem. He is not ready to take up the plow nor wait patiently for us to bring prosperity and harmony to each village. He also understands that as a married man, my wife is foremost in my heart, and my contribution to the overthrow of the invader will have to succeed one village at a time.

"Mary and I will miss you terribly," I tell him. My heart is in my throat and I cannot think of any thoughts worthy of how deeply my love is for him. Coughing out a few words as my tears well up, I can only say, "Be safe, and go with God."

He laughs at me, "Go with God?"

Considering the many conversations we have had about the corruption of the priests, and the endless number of false prophets we have mocked, my sentiment sounds out of character. Still, I want him to be careful more than anything.

"When has God ever helped us with anything?" asks Judas.

As if to mock me, Judas challenges the Almighty, blasphemy be damned. He looks skyward, then spreads his arms wide, and asks for help. "When will you finally come down from your heavenly realm, oh Great One, and help us slay these infidels! If you will not do that, at least let us be!"

Judas patiently waits for an army of angels to respond to his call, and when a thunderbolt does not strike him dead, he laughs and spits on the ground.

"At least be safe," asks Mary. "You know where to find us, either here or at the market. Visit us, please?"

"I will be on the lookout for you whenever I can, but lying low and striking quickly will be my new occupation. You two will always be in my thoughts."

Judas gives Mary a warm, loving hug, and tells her to please keep an eye on me. "He is on his own now. There will be no Judas to bail him out of trouble should any arise."

Judas turns away from us and departs without looking back. Mary and I both know his behavior only hides his emotional state. We are certain tears will be flowing once he is far enough away from the village. With a walking staff, gold coins, a bag of clothing, and a sheep's bladder filled with wine, he makes his way past the vineyards, orchards, and pastures, and enthusiastically greets everyone in the fields as he walks away at a brisk pace.

Mary and I walk to the edge of the wall and watch him as he travels down the long pathway. At the road, he turns and calls out, "If you need me, do not hesitate to send me a message!"

Occasionally, he turns to give us a wave. We watch him for as long as we can until he becomes a speck in the distance.

A year has passed since we first arrived in Bethlehem. Today, as I enter my twentieth year it is also Matthew's wedding day. Friends and family have worked hard to make it an event worthy of a remarkable young man and his bride. The square is filled with baskets of flowers, while dozens of torches surround the square, and numerous candles light the tables.

A noisy crowd ills the square with conversation and laughter while accompanied by music from local young men playing drums, flutes and stringed instruments. Matthew and his bride, Martha as they move through the large number of guests, and stopping to exchange conversation and good wishes from friends and family.

When they stop before us, they thank us for our efforts to make this wedding day a memorable and festive one and ask a simple request of me. "We have signed the wedding contract but we would like to have you bless our marriage," asks Matthew.

I am extremely flattered as I guessed that Eron would be

assigned the honor. "Of course I will, but you are already blessed. Look how many have gathered to wish you success and happiness. I pray that you are granted eternal happiness and comfort."

Matthew pulls Martha close to him and kisses her gently on the lips. Mary and I turn to each other with a sly conspiratorial smile as we know what takes place once the marriage contract between the families has been signed—when the couple is free to begin their new lives as husband and wife.

Martha looks into Matthew's eyes with a new appreciation of the joys of marriage. "I had always hoped to be blessed with a kind and caring husband; one who would be a good provider," she swoons. "But did not know that such passion existed with what I feel with Matthew."

Slow to realize what she has just implied, she blushes and buries her head into Matthew's chest. For his part, Matthew grins widely, and unable to hold in our amusement any longer, Mary and I burst out laughing.

I notice when Judas enters and stops in front of a group of young men gathered on the far side of the square, I assume my friend is entertaining them with tales of his latest exploits in Jerusalem when they all laugh too loudly at his stories—a boastful show of camaraderie and manliness. But in truth, it is a youthful game of flirting for the unattached young girls standing nearby giggling a them.

By his clothing, it appears Jerusalem has been a prosperous venture for him. He finally saunters over to us and laughs. "What a crowd—the cream of Bethlehem and the young dogs. This should be an interesting evening!"

Judas gives me a long studying look and says, "Why, you are quite a handsome young man. I do not think I have ever seen you not covered in dust and grime!"

Eron makes his way to the center of the courtyard and quietly asks the musicians to stop playing. "Friends! Friends! Your attention, please!" he announces.

We obediently turn our attention to him and wait patiently while he clears his throat, adjusts his tunic, and then clears his throat again. From a table of older women sitting in the shade of the old olive tree, Eron's wife moans. "Please husband, sometime today!"

Everyone laughs, and some of the town elders join in to hurl a few humorous insults. Eron holds his hand up to silence us and clears his throat once again.

"Many of you have traveled great distances to celebrate the joining of these two fine young people. I want to thank you from my heart, for we are blessed to be able to share in their happiness and our families' mutual good fortune!"

Eron retrieves a slatted wooden cage with six white doves and lays it on a low table. He holds his hands up for the guests to quiet, then looks around to those in attendance, many of who lived through the dark period of this town when Herod took the lives of their children.

"We have gathered before Matthew and Martha to celebrate their love, a mighty power that lightens every burden. Love bears every hardship as though it were nothing and renders all bitterness sweet and acceptable. Nothing is sweeter than love, nothing stronger, nothing more pleasant, nothing fuller or better on earth. May love shine down and bless them with a life filled with love, good health, and comfort."

Jesus opens the door of the cage and turns to the guests to announce, "Today is a joyful one and we will not join in nor be a part of the killing of any of God's creatures for the unholy practice of sacrifice."

A quiet gasp emits from some of the guests, possibly some thinking he has spoken blasphemy.

The doves cautiously waddle out of the cage one by one onto the table, a bit confused and curious at the many eyes staring at them.

Eron encourages them to make haste and leave. "Go," he tells them quietly.

Whether or not they understand his words, they lift off in unison and take flight, scattering in all directions. Their initial spontaneous outburst ends when they return to the square in formation. Seeing this, the wedding party cheers when the birds simultaneously land on the ancient olive tree and settle in to watch the rest of the ceremony from their leafy perch.

With the blessing complete, Eron announces, "You may have noticed the incredible aromas emanating from the kitchens. We praise God for blessing us this day with a bountiful harvest and give praise our brothers and sisters for their generous efforts in providing us with enough to celebrate this union for many hours. Please, let us give thanks to the Almighty for our good fortune. Let us eat!"

A loud applause is followed by Eron encouraging all to move to the large tables laden with meats, fish, bread, fruit, cheese, and jugs of wine. Happy to cooperate, the wedding guests move to the tables and we fill our plates.

Servers begin pouring wine and the musicians start up again. They play a song with a unique rhythm, popular with us younger people, much to the dismay of the older guests who would prefer a more sober celebration, or no music at all.

A young woman joins the musicians and quiets the crowd when she begins singing a haunting melody, perfectly fitting in with the rhythms being played.

Matthew polishes off the wine in his cup and takes Martha by the hand to an open space in the center of the tables. There, he pulls her to him and embraces her, followed by a long kiss, oblivious to the stares of others before they begin dancing close, lost in their wedded bliss,

Other couples to follow suit. Mary takes my hand, and we join them in the dance. We lock our arms into theirs and step in rhythm to the music. Guests of all ages enter the dance, and soon Matthew and Martha are forced into the center of the ring. As we circle them, they playfully but unsuccessfully attempt to break free from their confinement.

The band is possessed, playing with an intensity they might have never achieved before. We enthusiastically try to keep up with them as we are able, while Matthew and Martha continue attempting to break free of the circle. Each time they try, we push them back into the center. The circle is now spinning wildly out of control, with old and young alike laughing like children. There are no worries at this moment—crops in need of picking, roofs to be repaired, or animals to be fed are troubles better left for another time. This is a special day.

Older guests fall out of the circle and return to their tables, red-faced, winded, and happy. Within a few minutes, even Mary and I stumble off the dance floor and find an empty spot against a stone wall to catch our breath. I hold Mary close and stroke her hair and our deep breathing turns into an erotic game as we breathe in and out in cadence, feeling the heat of our bodies.

The sky is turning red as the sun begins to set and I take in a deep breath and detect the fragrance of Persian roses in Mary's hair. I feel the contours of her soft hips and small waist pressed against me and I wonder if one day she will bear a child, or might the question be; how many children will we have?

Mary sighs as she watches Matthew and Martha. "They are such a beautiful couple."

Martha breaks away from the circle and runs to us, laughing, panting, and nearly out of breath. She takes hold of our arms and attempts to pull us back to the dance. "Come you two, the celebration is just beginning!" she laughs. "You must join us!"

I resist, but Martha easily pulls an enthusiastic Mary from my arms as I watch her long hair flow over my outstretched hands as she leaves, and I feel tears of joy well-up in my eyes. Such is love.

The music has transported the exuberant dancers to another level—a rapture with all moving to the pulsating rhythms of the music. I watch Mary disappear before my eyes and merges with faces and bodies to become one laughing, whirling blur.

The dancing maelstrom makes my head spin, forcing me to turn away from the dancing to a group of village Elders sitting at a nearby table deep in discussion.

Eron takes notice of me, and smiles acknowledgment with a nod before turning back to the men at his table.

"Our beloved young man and his wife will be leaving us soon," says Erin. "I am told they will be venturing out into the harsh world of murders and robberies—the world into which he was born and to where he will now return."

"Praise God and protect him!" replies an elder.

One of the men, a grizzled farmer hisses, "What kind of plan calls for us to sit by and wait for a so-called savior while we suffer under the yoke of the Roman bastards?"

Eron replies, "Always the doubter. Even now with the child back in our village, you still question everything."

An elder sitting next to the farmer replies, "David, Isaiah, and Jeremiah predicted events that came to pass many years after they were proclaimed! Is that not proof of a divine plan? It is written. What else holds us together as a people?"

The farmer shakes his head and responds. "Then why have our many conquerors been rewarded so greatly while we toil away, waiting? When I ask, will this happen?"

"When men open their hearts and let Him in," replies Eron.

The Elders jolt in surprise as a drinking glass shatters and followed by a loud cheer. A trumpet and saxophone join the traditional instruments, and an electric guitar begins to produce a fast-paced run of notes soaring above pulsating rhythms.

Four young wedding guests surprise the Elders at the table holding cocktails in stemmed glassware and gather around a table. Two of the women wear modern evening gowns, while their dates are dressed in dark suits, white shirts and ties.

A village Elder also called the Mayor, glances at these new guests, tugs at his tunic, and turns his attention to the dance floor to watch the bridal couple. "How happy the bride looks in her white wedding gown," he says. " I pray these two can sustain their love in these troubling times.

Interrupting the Mayor, the young male guest exhales smoke from his cigarette, and says, "I couldn't help but overhear your discussion. The Bible tells us that God became flesh through Jesus Christ. That is correct, isn't it?"

The grizzled farmer shrugs and replies, "That story was

written three hundred years after the crucifixion by people who weren't even there."

The young guest's cheeks flush red—it's obvious to the older men at the table that he wears his religion close to the surface.

"Do you deny the existence of the Holy Trinity?" demands the young man.

"I ask you this," replies the farmer. "Why would God need to become flesh?"

"To tell the world that the Kingdom of God was at hand and to repent their sins!" answers the young man.

"And he did this by descending to Earth as a lowly man in some forgotten village at the end of the world? Isn't the miracle of life itself good enough for you?"

The young man leans in with his voice, which has become more aggressive even though respecting one's elders is important if one considers themselves to be a good Christian. "He took the form of Jesus Christ to teach and counsel man—to teach peace and respect for one another!"

The young woman who appears to be the man's date chimes in. "Jesus taught us that God is loving and He is in all things. Do you not accept the one true God? The creator of heaven and earth?"

A response to her question is never given as the loud music finally ends, much to the dismay of the crowd who moan in jest of their displeasure before applauding.

The Mayor pushes his chair away from the table and stands to face the young guests. He holds up the palms of his hands to signal this useless eternal argument. His participation in the discussion has come to an end. Before he turns to leave, he tells the young couple, "If what you say is true, then there has never been such a tale of wonder and magic since the beginning of time."

Without warning, six white doves suddenly take flight from the ancient olive tree overlooking the party. They swoop low over an old stone wall and startle a watchdog who barks out a warning, too late to be of any help except to watch them gracefully descend the steep hillside and over the wedding guests' cars lining the road below.

The doves quickly cross over a field of wheat, a vineyard, and a neatly tended orchard. If one cared to follow their journey, as is the watchdog, they would see the doves fly straight into the setting sun sitting directly over the massive, glistening dome of Jerusalem's Golden Temple.

A VERY SPECIAL DAY

The cool night air swirls overhead as Evan and Holly sit low in Evan's sports car, hunkered down in the convertible on a narrow road winding its way through low hills filled with coastal oaks. The road drops them into a valley filled with dormant vineyards and they pass a dilapidated barn leaning dangerously off to one side as it mimics a twisted ancient apple tree standing nearby. The barn's function ended years ago when the apple orchard was dug up and replaced by vineyards. No longer needed to house ladders and apple crates, its historical charm has kept it from destruction until it collapsed on its own accord.

They turn off the road onto Eden Valley Road and catch the first view of Christine and Mark's estate looming over the valley at the top of the road with strings of white lights encircling the roof's outline.

"What a cool spot!" exclaims Holly. "Eden Valley Road. That's so appropriately named."

Evan nods in agreement and says, "I've spent many hours driving this road, and you'd think with all the money up in this area, they would repair the potholes."

"It gives the place character," laughs Holly. "So, this is your first visit since you attacked Mimi. Are you gonna be okay?"

Evan shakes his head and laughs. "Well, when you put it that way, I'm not so sure. But yeah, we've put all that behind us, thanks to you straightening my head out."

"It's been lots of fun," replies Holly, "and once you stopped drinking, I found out why she liked you in the first place. I think she blew it."

"Thanks! Although, if I hadn't been such a drunk, we would have never met." Evan laughs. "Wow, that sounded terrible. Let's not use that story if anyone asks how we met. Anyway, I'm glad it's you by my side."

Evan leans over, and kisses Holly on the cheek.

"Aww, it's mutual, I'm sure," she gushes.

Holly and Evan are on their way to Christine and Mark's annual Christmas Day bash. Now that Evan is out of the doghouse, he and Holly have even become friends with Mimi and her boyfriend, Tim. It's been a long year for all of them, but with sobriety, school, and a growing love for each other, the dark days of the past are a slowly fading memory.

Sidney and I are greeted in the courtyard by a thousand white roses in giant urns and music from a trio of musicians playing ancient instruments. The music and the atmosphere send us back in time to ancient Persia. Before we enter the house a young woman wearing black slacks and a starched white shirt with a bow tie hands us a glass of champagne.

The line of guests entering the foyer has run into a bit of gridlock because a young couple has stopped in front of *Jesus, The Teenage Years and are* studying it closely. I recognize the young man as Mimi's old boyfriend Evan, who is holding hands with a pretty young woman whom I don't think I've ever seen before at any of these parties. She seems to be captivated by the painting, and I guess this might be the young woman's first look at it. I'm also stunned to see more lipstick marks than ever on the painting's glass. It appears that a ritual has developed with women visitors planting a kiss on the glass for good luck.

Evan looks away from the painting, and when he makes eye contact with us he nods and smiles. He pulls the girl he's with away from the painting and he offers us his hand. "Hi, David. Hi Sidney!"

We shake hands and ask him how he's been.

"I'm doing well, David, thanks for asking. It's great to see you guys again."

Sidney gives him a big hug and a friendly kiss on the cheek. "We're so proud of you. Christina told us you're on your way to becoming a fireman."

"Yeah, it's been a long road. I start my first day on the job in less than two weeks."

"That is great news! Congratulations," exclaims Sidney.

"Thanks, your opinion means a lot to me," replies Evan and gently pulls Holly to him. "David, my girlfriend has been anxious to meet you ever since we got the invite. I think you might have another fan of Teenage Jesus."

Evan's girlfriend thrusts out her hand so quickly that it makes me flinch. For a second, I think she's got a gun or a knife. I guess I'm not over having an entire religious cult wanting to kick my ass.

"Hi, I'm Holly!" she says enthusiastically.

"Hi, Holly. I'm David. It's a pleasure to meet you."

Holly steps in close and looks into my eyes, then wraps her arms tightly around my waist, and buries her head into my chest. This seems to be a very emotional moment for her, but I'm confused too, because I've never had a response like this to any of my art.

I glance at Sidney to see her shaking her head with a sly smile. I know this is going to be one of those moments she'll bring up in the future; like the time she watched me get propositioned by a prostitute in a bar who I thought was a nurse until she began bringing up her husband's prostate problem.

I ask Holly, "Is everything okay?"

She replies with a long exhale, "I'm sorry. I just got a little overwhelmed meeting you. Your painting means a lot to me." When Holly releases me from her embrace, she takes my hands in hers, looks into my eyes with the most sincere expression, and says quietly, "You are a good person."

An hour later the dance floor is packed with couples doing rock-a-billy swing dance moves to a rocking version of Well, All Right, by Buddy Holly. The music echoes throughout the house and out over the valley. Many of the guests sound as if they might have already had a good fill of Christmas cheer as they sing mostly out of key along with the song's chorus.

Well all right, well all right
Our lifetime of love will be all right.
Well all right, well all right,
We can live and love with all our might.

Sidney and I leave the singing and dancing and escape outside for some fresh air. Of course, I have to stop on our way out and take another look at, *Jesus, The Teenage Years*. I love the lipstick graffiti surrounding the spray-painted message of "Heresy," especially in all the different colors. From bright pink to deep red. There are even a few black lipstick marks left over from Halloween.

I laugh as I look at the hostile graffiti message which is now greatly outnumbered by the statements of affection.

"I wonder how the vandals would react now seeing all that blasphemy?"

Sidney places a kiss on the glass and says, "I hear it brings good luck. By the way, what do you think about Evan's girlfriend hugging you like that? What brought that on?"

I think about it for a moment before shrugging, "I don't know. I guess just I'm a good person."

We stroll the lush gardens under the arbor lit with hundreds of white lights and enter the brick courtyard overlooking the valley to see the ocean far in the distance shimmering like a jewel. The evening's colorful display of winter clouds that had threatened to put a damper on the party earlier are turning gold, red, and in some shadowed areas, a deep purple. Awestruck, we embrace and watch the clouds change colors with each passing moment.

"God, this is incredible," sighs Sidney.

"I can't imagine anything else to make this a more magical moment," I add.

But, what happens next does exceed our imagination when a half dozen white doves pass overhead in formation, dropping and climbing for no apparent reason or as their leader sees fit.

Holding our embrace we follow the flight of the doves as they pass over the hilltop estate with its roof covered with hundreds of twinkling lights decorated to celebrate either the winter solstice or the birth of a baby boy born in a barn over two thousand years ago.

The rise and fall of Eden Valley's terrain dictates the doves' flight path as they hug the tops of pistachio and olive trees, rows of vineyards, then over a dilapidated barn being kept company by an ancient apple tree. Upon reaching the ridge of the surrounding hills they vanish from sight into the glowing rays of the setting sun on this very special day.

ABOUT THE AUTHOR

Tom Trujillo is an artist and writer living in Central California with his wife of many years and are the parents of two adult children and two grandchildren. *Heresy: Jesus, The Teenage Years*, is Tom's first novel and his fourth published book.

Tom has spent his professional life as an illustrator and graphic designer with an extensive portfolio of over forty years designing book covers, magazines, package designs, exhibits, and trade shows. His paintings have been exhibited in various group art shows, Santa Cruz County Open Studios, and a one-man exhibit at the Museum of Art & History of Santa Cruz. Many of his paintings are found in several private collections.

PHOTOGRAPH BY KIM TRUJILLO

OTHER BOOKS BY TOM TRUJILLO

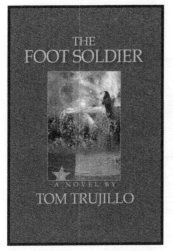

In 1967, the Summer of Love and the Magical Mystery Tour met Mississippi Burning and the Vietnam War in a small Texas town—What could go wrong?

A labor organizer for Tejano and Mexican farm workers is beaten and lynched after a labor strike. From the noose, the man in the tree vows to avenge his death, and with the aid of Mescalito and an ancient Mexican cowboy spirit, his prayers set in motion an intricate series of encounters. Two hippies leave San Francisco and travel to Texas to counsel young men to avoid the draft and the Vietnam War, and what they discover is another war being waged in their own country—the war on brown skin. Life unfolds, plans change, and the man in the tree receives the revenge he had been praying for.

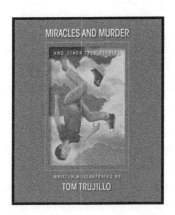

A fully illustrated collection of Tom's true-life adventures accompanied by dozens of his colorful illustrations. Tom's stories weave their way through a life of wrangling back rent out of a murdering motorcycle gang, alien abduction, escaping a vicious dog thanks to the appearance of a tall metal pole in the middle of a stream, thoughts on butterflies, irony, and of course, miracles and his first murder. These entertaining, inspiring, and humorous tales are carefully and lovingly recounted in the tradition of American folklore and Texas tall tales.

Whoa, wheeee, what a ride! Thank you Tom. Your book was a joy to read and your artwork is fantastic! It was a sad day when I finished reading the last of your stories. Kind of like saying goodbye to a fun evening of feasting with friends. I look forward to more books...love your sensitivity and your consistent voice. So many fun adventures and I can only imagine you have a ton more up your sleeve. Emily Bording

THE DETOUR

TOM TRUJILLO

A SCIENCE FICTION NOVEL

Three million years ago, a race known as Celestins traveled to a barren planet in search of water and accidentally ripped open the crust and released billions of tons of lava, boiling mud, and bacteria. The eruption destroyed their equipment and nearly destroyed the Celestin engineers. It was a complete failure, and they returned to their home planet empty-handed.

One million years later, the Celestins returned to repair the damage only to find the "accident" had created Earth as we know it with fresh air, clean water, and life. A group of 400 Celestins, our ancient ancestors, set out to explore and settle the planet and build settlements. As magnificent as this planet was, it was also a cruel, violent existence. The gentle soul of the Celestins was no match for the beasts and poisonous plants that had evolved on Earth in perfection. Over time, they hardened to evolve into humans; violent, cruel, and uncaring for their fellow man.

Today, the Celestins have returned to save the Earth from centuries of destructive human activity that has brought civilization to the brink of destruction because of global climate change caused by pollution.

Dr. Ron Fisher and thousands of others are taken aboard Celestin ships to assist them in destroying carbon dioxide polluters, such as the oil industry, before life on Earth ceases to exist. The saboteurs are shown how to blast a chemical into pipelines to turn the oil into a new compound capable of providing clean energy for eternity. The Celestins reward Dr. Fisher and others with the gift of "The Touch," which spreads quickly, and a new World is created—free of pollution, one of compassion and peace, and bringing to an end all wars and greed.

Made in the USA
Las Vegas, NV
22 September 2024

95513468R10142